CW00410461

DIRTY WORDS (A MFM MENAGE ROMANCE)

TARA CRESCENT

Text copyright © 2017 Tara Crescent
All Rights Reserved

No part of this book may be reproduced in any form or by any electronic or mechanical means including information storage and retrieval systems, without permission in writing from the author. The only exception is by a reviewer, who may quote short excerpts in a review.

This book is a work of fiction. Names, characters, places, and incidents either are products of the author's imagination or are used fictitiously. Any resemblance to actual persons, living or dead, events, or locales is entirely coincidental.

My editor Jim takes the comma-filled words that emerge from my keyboard and shapes it into a story worth reading. As always, my undying gratitude.

Additional thanks for Miranda's laser-sharp eyes.

Cover Design by Kasmit Covers

FREE STORY OFFER

Get a free story when you subscribe to <u>my mailing list!</u>

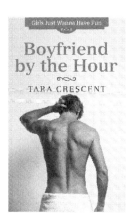

Boyfriend by the Hour

This steamy, romantic story contains a dominant hero who's pretending to be an escort, and a sassy heroine who's given up on real relationships.

Sadie:

I can't believe I have the hots for an escort.

Cole Mitchell is ripped, bearded, sexy and dominant. When he moves next door to me, I find it impossible to resist sampling the wares.

But Cole's not a one-woman kind of guy, and I won't share.

Cole:

She thinks I'm an escort. I'm not.

I thought I'd do anything to sleep with Sadie. Then I realized I want more. I want Sadie. Forever.

I'm not the escort she thinks I am.

Now, I just have to make sure she never finds out.

DIRTY WORDS

If you're going to write dirty stories about your neighbors, don't give them tiny cocks.

Love thy neighbors? No way. *Never going to happen.*

Ethan Burke and Lars Johansen are **chiseled** male perfection, with their **cocky** smiles, **bulging** biceps and **washboard abs.**

They're also **rich, arrogant** jerks. *Ugh.*

I'm supposed to **swoon** over their panty-melting smiles, **but I refuse to get the memo.** After we feud over a parking spot, I write them into a dirty story.

And, when it comes to describing their, ahem, **equipment,** I get very stingy. How stingy? **Think two inches.**

Bad author.

Unfortunately for me, they **find** the story.

And they make me **read** it to them. While showing me how **wrong** I was. *One deliciously long inch at a time.*

For the record - they're **very** well endowed.

I've never been happier to write a retraction.

1

MAGGIE

The red Lamborghini is in my parking spot again.

Evidently, if you own a fancy car, you don't have to act like a civilized human being.

I'm ready to lose my shit. *Stupid, self-centered, entitled, smug billionaires,* I mutter to myself, irritated beyond belief. My new neighbors, Ethan Burke and Lars Johansen might be easy on the eyes, but no amount of hotness is going to stop me from getting the overpriced Italian sports car towed.

Life Rule Number 45: Don't park in a spot that's marked Reserved, unless it's actually reserved *for you.*

Look, I'm not a jerk. The first day the car was in my spot, I rolled my eyes and parked in the large lot two blocks down from the restaurant. *Maybe they didn't see the sign that said 'Reserved for China Garden,'* I thought charitably. *Don't make a big deal of it, Maggie.*

My patience slipped the second time around, but I'd gritted my teeth and left a tersely worded note under the wiper blades.

You're in my parking space. The sign that says 'Reserved' isn't a suggestion. Might I suggest brushing up on your reading comprehension skills?

Okay, fine. The note was cranky, but can you really blame me? Just because the two billionaires are getting their parking lot resurfaced doesn't give them the right to high-handedly park in my space. They could have done the neighborly thing by asking for permission, but of course, they didn't. They've assumed that because they're richer than God, they can just do whatever they want.

Not this time, dickwads.

My arms are laden with groceries, and to add insult to injury, it's raining. The cold, damp drizzle gets under my skin and chills my bones. It's supposed to be spring, but the weather doesn't seem to get the memo. By the time I get back into my apartment, my clothes are soaked, I'm shivering with cold, and I'm fuming. Normally, I'm not a confrontational person, but today, I'm calling parking enforcement, and I'm getting the Lamborghini towed.

I dial Joe Laramie's number. "Joe," I tell the cop when he picks up his phone, "The billionaires' obnoxious sports car is in my parking spot." My voice rises with frustration. "I had to park in the downtown overflow lot again. I'm cold, I'm miserable, and I want to throw a rock through the windshield. Do something."

Joe chuckles good-naturedly. The big, burly policeman went to high school with me and is one of my best friends. We even went to prom together one year, though when we kissed at the end of the night, it had felt like kissing my brother. *Ick.* After that, our relationship has remained friendly and warm but strictly platonic. "No need to damage property, tiger cat," he says, amusement in his voice. "I'll be right there."

ETHAN BURKE AND LARS JOHANSEN are New Summit's newest residents, and ever since they moved in a month ago, everyone in town has been breathless with curiosity about the two men.

According to Google, they founded a cutting-edge media company while they were still in college. Last year, they sold it to a large California tech giant for three billion dollars, leaving both men with roughly a billion dollars each, and the Internet is rife with speculation about what the men are planning to do next.

At first, I'd been excited about the prospect of new neighbors, especially neighbors with enough money to restore the crumbling brick building opposite me to its former glory. The Morris-Stanton building is an eyesore, with broken windows, peeling paint and a general air of neglect. Scores of prospective tenants have toured the place, but they've all been scared off by the extensive renovations required to render the long-vacant hotel habitable. So when the building was sold last year, and crews descended on the place to fix it up, I was thrilled.

When it became apparent that my new neighbors were very pretty eye-candy, and I had a clear view of their main living space from my bedroom opposite the street, I was even more delighted.

Of course, I should have known that it was all too good to be true. You don't become a billionaire by the time you're thirty by being nice. You do it by riding roughshod over everyone else, and by paying no attention to rules and regulations. Including signs about reserved parking spots.

So much for your dirty fantasies, Maggie.

I shower quickly, turning the handle to scalding and soaking in the warmth. I'm feeling much better by the time I head downstairs. While I was in the shower, it's stopped raining, and the sun's come out after three days of non-stop drizzle. I'm *almost* tempted to tell a grinning Joe Laramie that I don't care about the stupid Lamborghini.

One of the billionaires is outside as well, talking on the phone, a frown on his face. Joe nods in his direction. "You could just go tell him to move his car, Mags," he says peaceably.

"It's not his car," I reply shortly. "Ethan drives a Land Rover. This is Lars' car."

Joe's eyebrows rise. "Lars, is it?" he drawls teasingly. "Maggie May, allow me to give you a bit of friendly guy advice. If you want to hit on a guy, don't get his car towed. Men can get a little bit obsessive about their wheels." He gives the cherry red sports car that's currently in my parking spot an appreciative look. "Especially one as beautiful as this baby."

From across the street, Ethan's eyes flicker over to the two of us. Joe lifts up his hand in a friendly wave, and Ethan nods curtly.

Life Rule Number 3: Don't lust after jerks.

Asshole. Probably thinks he's too good for this town. My resolve hardens at the dismissive gesture. "I'm not interested in either of them," I say, lying through my teeth. "I think they're inconsiderate jerks, and this car is *definitely* parked in my spot. I want it towed."

Joe shakes his head but pulls out his phone. "Alright," he says, "On your head be it. I'll call Tom. But Mags, these guys are your neighbors. Do you really want to be at war with them?"

Out of the corner of my eye, I see a sodden piece of paper under the wiper blade of Lars Johansen's sports car. It's my note. The jerk hasn't even bothered reading it.

It's time for war.

"Tow it," I say flatly.

2

LARS

After a year of being one of the idle rich, I'm going out of my mind with boredom, and more than ready to start a new venture. This time, in publishing.

ReadStream's idea is simple. We want to create stories with the depth of a book, and the interactive experience of a really good video game. I'm convinced that the next wave of innovation in the publishing world will involve books with enhanced reading experiences, and the Big Five are too busy protecting their existing business that they're unwilling to embrace change. New York is stagnant, desperate, and dying.

Which brings me to today's meeting with Helena Wu. Helena's an agent representing Cara Sandoval-Nez, who's written a beautiful, lush fantasy novel set in an alternate America, one undiscovered by Christopher Columbus.

Renee, my Editorial Director, has been pushing hard for us to acquire this novel to be our first project, and she's right. Now, I just have to convince the skeptical agent that we're the best house for her client's novel.

I'm expecting it to be something of an uphill battle—we're an upstart publisher, and word on the street is that three New York publishers are bidding hard for the book.

Sure enough, Helena's opening statement is not encouraging. "Mr. Johansen," she says, giving me a piercing look through her black-rimmed glasses, "do you know how many new publishing companies fail?"

Across from me, Ethan bites back a grin. I thought Helena's first question would be a softball; Ethan predicted that the longtime agent would go for the jugular. I owe him fifty bucks.

"Ninety percent of them fail in the first two years," I reply. "I've done my research, Ms. Wu. Let me tell you why ReadStream is different, and why I believe we're the best publisher for 'A Land Filled with Raven Song.'"

We're well on our way to making our case when Ethan's phone rings. He glances at the display and leaves the room with a muttered apology. Which means the call's from Ethan's crazy ex-wife, Catalina.

Sighing inwardly, I return to the pitch. Catalina pushed hard for the divorce two years ago, but the moment the company was sold for billions, she's taken to phoning Ethan every other day. I've told my best friend to block her number a million times, but Ethan has one weak spot, and that's his supermodel ex-wife.

After forty-five minutes of discussion, I think we've nailed it. Renee and I have convinced Helena of ReadSteam's value proposition, and let's be honest, the half-a-million dollar advance we're willing to offer Cara Sandoval-Nez doesn't hurt.

"I'll take your offer to Cara," Helena promises us. "Of course, she'll be making the final decision, but I'm sure she'll be impressed by what ReadStream is offering."

We're just getting up and shaking hands when Ethan reenters the room. "You did clear it with the Chinese restaurant opposite the street that you're parking there, right?" he asks me.

"Yes," I reply, puzzled. "You were there when I chatted with Dominic last week. We spent almost an hour talking about cars. Why?"

Ethan's eyes dance with glee. "Because they're towing the Lambo," he replies. "I think you should go rescue your baby, Lars."

3

ETHAN

Okay, fine. I admit I'm a little too amused by this situation, but honestly, Lars is such a baby about his collection of Lamborghinis that I can't resist. Two days ago, he got snippy with me because I ate a French fry in his car. *One fucking French fry.* I don't understand this kind of obsessiveness. I drive a Land Rover that will take all the abuse I can throw at it. As far as I'm concerned, a car is a tool to get you from Point A to Point B.

Besides, it serves Lars right for ignoring that note.

I told my buddy to get the misunderstanding sorted out right away. Yes, Dominic Zhang told him it was okay to park there, but as far as I can tell, the young man doesn't live on site, his older sister Maggie does.

After yet another long bitch-fest from Catalina, this time lasting forty-five *fucking* minutes, I'm in need of some cheering up, so I follow Lars downstairs, ready to watch the circus unfold. The tow-truck has pulled up in front of the restaurant, and a big guy is slipping a pair of dollies under the front wheels of Lars' pride and joy.

This is going to be good.

"What the heck are you doing?" Lars bolts across the street, his voice rising in panic. "Are you trying to destroy my transmission?"

The tow truck driver stops what he's doing, and shrugs helplessly. He seems a little relieved not to have to tow the car. "Not too many Lamborghini's in this town," he says. "I'm doing the best I can."

To Lars' credit, he's not a total dick, so he doesn't vent at the tow truck driver. He turns, instead, to the cop. "I'm Lars Johansen," he introduces himself. "This is my car. Can you tell me what the problem is?"

When I was downstairs earlier, listening to Catalina complain about something or the other, I saw Maggie Zhang talk to the cop, but now, when she steps out of the doorway, I notice her for the first time.

She's absolutely gorgeous.

I've stopped by the China Garden for takeout before; I've seen Maggie there, her hair pinned back in a neat bun, her body enveloped in a white chef's apron. Sometimes she works in the front, and other times, she's in the kitchen, but I've never paid her much attention. She's always been part of the scenery.

I'm a fool.

Her hair hangs loose down her shoulders, damp tendrils curling around her face. Her lips are soft and pink, her face scrubbed free of makeup. She's clearly not wearing a bra underneath her gray t-shirt, and I swear I can see the outline of her nipples against the thin fabric.

"The problem," she says, marching up to Lars, her chin tilted up and her eyes flashing with irritation, "is that you're in my parking spot for the third time in four days."

Lars gives her an incredulous look. "I live across the street from you," he bites out. "You couldn't come knock on the door and ask me to move it? You called a tow truck instead?"

She folds her hands over her chest, and the movement pushes her perky little breasts up. I'm aware that I'm staring at them like a teenage boy, but I can't help myself. How the heck did I not notice how beautifully lush Maggie Zhang is?

"It's not my responsibility to ensure that you're following parking restrictions, Mr. Johansen," she snaps.

Lars gets on his knees and carefully examines his car. "My paint is scratched," he says, running his fingers down the side of his car. He glares at Maggie. "I should send you the bill."

"You can try," she snarls. "And I'll treat it the same way you treated my note."

As entertaining as this is, it's time for me to intervene. I cross the street and stick out my hand in greeting. "I'm Ethan Burke." I give Maggie my best charming smile. "There's been some kind of misunderstanding."

Up close, Maggie's even prettier than she was from across the street, and even more irritated. "The only misunderstanding I can see," she says coldly, "is that you think that being rich gives you the license to do whatever you want, without regard for the consequences."

My temper rises at this infuriatingly unfair accusation. This is the kind of shit that Catalina was skilled at doing during our two years of marriage, and I've just about had it with tempestuous women. "If you talk to your brother," I snap at her, "you'll find out that he told Lars that it was perfectly okay for him to park his car there while our lot was getting resurfaced."

Maggie's lips form a small 'O.'

"Dominic told you to park here?" the cop asks, turning to Maggie with a rueful grimace. "Yeah, that sounds like him alright. Looks like he forgot to tell you about the arrangement, Mags."

Maggie's face heats with embarrassment. "Sorry," she says stiffly to Lars. "I should have checked." She bites her lower lip, her teeth indenting the soft flesh in a way that I find difficult to resist. "I'll pay for the scratch to be fixed."

Without another word, she turns around and heads back inside. The cop raises an eyebrow at us. "Welcome to New Summit, gentlemen," he says. "I'm Joe Laramie. The tow truck driver here is Tom Ramirez, who also plows the roads in winter."

We shake hands cordially and prepare to leave. As we're crossing the street, Joe's voice stops us. "You're not planning to send Maggie a bill, are you?"

Lars turns around, a sheepish expression on his face. As predicted, my friend has calmed down and is feeling like a jerk. "No, of course not," he says. "I shouldn't have lost my cool."

Joe laughs. "Maggie's been known to have that effect on guys."

No kidding. I'm feeling a little dazed from our encounter and judging from the expression on Lars' face, I'm not the only one.

As we cross back to our office, I can't resist one more dig. "Maggie Zhang seems just your type," I point out slyly.

Lars knows what I'm doing, and doesn't fall for the bait. "I'm not about to start dating our neighbor," he says dryly. "Even if she *is* just my type." He gives me a sidelong look. "Besides, are you really in any position to talk, Ethan?" he snickers. "I noticed that you had to keep adjusting yourself. Attracted to Maggie, are we?"

I shrug. Nothing's going to come of it. After Catalina, I'm quite determined not to get involved with anyone seriously. Especially not our too-hot, too-temperamental neighbor.

4

MAGGIE

I f the ground would open and swallow me up, that'd be great.

Also, I'm going to kill my brother. Even if doing so would violate Life Rule Number 2: Do not lose your temper with your family.

As much as I'd like to stick around and wallow in my shame, I have a busy afternoon ahead of me. I don't work in our family restaurant on Wednesdays, and it's the day I do the bulk of my errands.

I'm about to head down the street when my mother beckons to me from the restaurant. I obediently detour inside. "What was all the shouting about?" she asks me.

"One of the guys across the street was parked in my spot," I mutter.

She nods immediately. "Yes, Dominic told them that was okay." She smiles fondly. "You know your brother. He likes fast cars."

"You knew, and you didn't tell me?" I shake my head, frustrated beyond belief. "I just made a complete ass of myself yelling at Lars Johansen, all because Dominic gave away my parking spot."

My mother frowns at me. "Don't get angry with your brother, Maggie May," she says sternly. "He's just a baby."

I roll my eyes. In the Zhang family dynamic, Dominic, the son, can do no wrong, and the daughters are supposed to be kind, gentle, and patient. It's no wonder my sister Lilly won't step back in New Summit, and it's no wonder I'm cranky. "Whatever," I say, feeling like a sullen teenager. "I'm going out. Do you need anything?"

"Are you going on a date?" she asks hopefully.

"Mom," I say with exasperation. "It's two in the afternoon. Who goes on a date at this time?"

"I do," she replies with a cheerful smile. "Patrick and I like to go for a walk in the park during the day. It's very nice."

Unable to help myself, I grin. For the first year after my dad died, my mother was grief-stricken and numb. I'm so glad she met Patrick. The two of them are adorable together, and as much as my mom drives me insane sometimes, I love her, and I'm really glad she's happy.

"I'm just doing errands, mom. But if I see an eligible man, I'll be sure to get his phone number."

I WAS a little evasive with my mother. I'm not out doing errands; I'm headed to the offices of Benjamin Long and Landon West.

Ben and Landon are somewhat notorious in New Summit. They're sex therapists. When they first moved to town, their occupation had scandalized the residents, who were afraid that their presence in New Summit was going to rain down sin and corruption on our idyllic town.

I'm not one of them. Ben and Landon have been in a relationship with Mia, one of my really good friends, for about two years, and they treat her like a princess. I like the two men, and consider them my friends.

Ben's reading something on his computer when I walk in, and Landon's eating a bar of chocolate. When they see me, they look somewhat surprised, which is fair, since I've never shown up at their workplace before. "Hey Maggie," Ben says, a quizzical look on his face, "what's up?"

"I'm not here socially," I reply nervously. "Can I talk to you about something?"

Landon looks uncomfortable. "Maggie, we can't see you professionally. You're our friend; it's pretty dodgy for us to counsel you."

"It's not about my sex life," I reassure them. Well, it is, but only indirectly. After three years back in New Summit, I'm restless and cranky, and I'm itching for a challenge, and I'm hoping that Ben and Landon can provide some neutral advice.

"Tell you what," Ben says. "Why don't you tell me what's going on, and if you need counseling, I'll recommend another therapist."

"Not Dr. Bollington," Landon quips.

"Okay." I enter Ben's office, shutting the door behind me, and take a seat on the overstuffed gray armchair. Ben sits across from me and gives me an encouraging smile. "What's bothering you?"

"Everything," I reply at once, and then take a deep breath and take a newspaper clipping out of my handbag and push it toward Ben. "My twin sister Lilly just became the sous-chef of Stone Soup. It's a modern Chinese restaurant in San Francisco." My lips twist into a grimace. "Stone Soup has two Michelin stars."

Ben gives me a questioning look. "I didn't know you had a twin," he says. "I've met your mother many times, and though Angela talks about Dominic and you all the time, she never mentions your sister."

I sigh. "They don't get along. Chinese family dynamics are a bit crazy."

He chuckles. "Everyone thinks their family dynamics are crazy. I assure you, it's not restricted to any particular ethnicity. Why don't they get along?"

"My parents had very definite ideas for their children. They wanted Dominic to be a doctor or a lawyer. Lilly and I were supposed to work in the family restaurant and inherit it when they died."

"I take it that Lilly didn't go along with that plan?"

"Neither of us did, at the start," I admit. "When we turned eighteen, we both left for the west coast and got jobs in San Francisco kitchens. We both loved to cook, but we didn't want to take over the China Garden."

"Then what happened?"

"My dad died unexpectedly." My throat tightens when I think of the phone call I received in the middle of the night, the one I'd never forget. "My mother was struggling to manage by herself, and Dominic was just eighteen. So I moved back home to help. Lilly didn't, and my mother resents her for it."

Landon surveys me keenly. "Are you sure you don't resent her too?" he asks. He taps the newspaper clipping I handed him. "She's living the life you wanted for yourself."

"I don't resent anyone." He opens his mouth, but I continue before he speaks. "I don't. Nobody forced me to move back home. I love my mother, and I have a duty to my family. I'd make the same choice again."

"Okay," he says. "Let's say I believe what you're saying. Why are you here?"

Ben's blunt question throws me. What do I want? I ignore the image of Lars Johansen and Ethan Burke that appears in my mind and give Ben's query serious consideration.

Do I want to uproot myself all over again, go back to San Francisco, share an astronomically priced studio apartment with Lilly and try to work my way up the ranks, as if the last three years never happened?

No. I don't want that.

Ethan Burke has dimples. When he'd smiled at me, his dark eyes twinkling, for a brief, insane second, I'd wanted to lick those dimples. And other bits of him.

And Lars? When he'd knelt, his fingers caressing his stupid car's paint, my insides had clenched.

God, I'm fucked up. Why on Earth would I be attracted to them? They're total dicks. Maybe I will accept Ben's suggestion for a therapist referral because I clearly need my head examined.

"Maggie?" Ben's voice interrupts my thoughts. "You still with me?"

My cheeks heat. "Yeah. Sorry." I take a deep breath and shove the two aggravating men out of my mind. "I don't know what I want, Ben. I don't want to leave New Summit, but at the same time, I can't see myself running China Garden for the rest of my life. I'm bored out of my mind cooking spring rolls, fried rice, and ma po tofu, and it isn't getting better."

"You can't change up the menu?"

I shake my head. "I've had this argument a thousand times with my mom, but I think she's right. China Garden fits a niche in this town. We cook tasty but generic Chinese food, and that's what our customers want. If I start experimenting, I'm afraid I'll ruin the business my parents built when they came to America."

Ben gives me a sympathetic look. "How about another creative outlet?" he asks. "Do you paint? Garden? Write?"

Hmm. Ben might have something here. I can't hold a paintbrush if my life depended on it, but writing might be fun. As kids, Lilly and I used to entertain ourselves by making up stories about the people in town. Perhaps I can capture some of that magic again.

I walk back home with a spring in my step. The Lamborghini is nowhere in sight, which is a good thing, given my general ire about the billionaires across the street. Heading upstairs to my apartment, I crack open my laptop and open a new document, but then I draw a blank. What am I supposed to write about?

Inspiration strikes when I look out of the window. The Morris-Stanton building is a four-story structure, with large arched windows. I can see clearly into what appears to be Lars Johansen's bedroom.

I watch him unbutton his shirt and shrug it off his shoulders. He's pacing back and forth, talking to someone on the phone, and every time he comes into view, I catch sight of his six-pack abs, and I swear, my nipples perk up.

Write something, Ben had suggested.

Hands on keyboard, I start typing. Ladies and gentlemen, it's smut o' clock.

B&J was something of a legend. From the outside, the spa, housed in a turn-of-the-century brick building, looked like any other massage parlor in town, but for those that knew the code, it offered more.

Maggie was in need of a happy ending.

"Welcome to B&J." The tall blond man who greeted her wore a white t-shirt that clung to his muscles and loose gray linen pants. "My name is Lars. How can I help you today?"

"I'm in need of some TLC," Maggie replied. "Your service came highly recommended."

His eyes raked over her body. His exploration was slow and leisurely, and when he met her eyes again, his expression was hungry. "I'm pleased to hear that," he replied, the polite words a counterweight to the fire in his eyes. "Which one of our services are you interested in?"

Be bold, Maggie, she told herself.

"Your two-masseuse special," she said. She was trying to sound bold and self-assured, but she couldn't stop the flush from spreading across her face.

His lips quirked. "Yes," he said, "I rather thought that might be it. Please come with me."

She followed him up a flight of stairs, and into a small windowless room. The air was heavy with the smells of jasmine and musk. Candles were everywhere, filling the space with flickering light. "Take off your clothes and lie down," Lars instructed, pointing to the massage table.

No 'please' this time. The instruction was definitely an order.

"Are you going to leave while I undress?" Maggie asked, a definite tremor in her voice.

"Why would I do that?"

With shaking fingers, Maggie stepped out of her too-short red skirt and lifted her tight black t-shirt over her head. The door opened while she was getting naked, and another man stepped into the room. "Hello," he said calmly. "I'm Ethan."

Lars was tall and blond. He reminded Maggie of Chris Hemsworth. Ethan was Loki to Lars' Thor. He was dark-haired and lean, stubble shadowing his cheeks, a wicked glint in his chocolate-brown eyes.

Ladies, Maggie thought to herself. *I get it now. I understand why B&J's special services are so popular.*

She lay down on the massage table, face down. The air was warm, but goosebumps still rose on her skin. "I'm going to start on your legs," Lars said. "Ethan will work on your upper half."

Warm liquid trickled down her spine and the back of her thighs and calves, pooling on the vinyl table. "What's your name?" Ethan asked her.

"Maggie," she murmured.

"Maggie, we're going to start gentle," Ethan said. "If you want us to go harder, please let us know. We're amenable to special requests."

He said *harder*, and her mind immediately thought about their cocks, thrusting into her, deep and firm. She pictured one of them fucking her pussy, while the other forced her to take him in her mouth. She imagined being overwhelmed, filled completely, gasping for breath, begging for them to pound faster...

Then Ethan moved in front of her, and placed his large hands on her back, spreading the oil over her flesh and kneading it in. His cock was inches from her mouth, and judging from the size of the bulge under his drawstring linen pants, he was hung like a horse. Or so it seemed. For all Maggie knew, he stuffed a sock down there.

His fingers trailed over the side of her breasts, but for the moment, he seemed content with teasing her.

Maggie almost licked her lips; she was that turned on.

While Ethan kneaded her upper back, Lars got to work

on her legs. His strong, capable palms glided over her thighs, and when he inched higher, Maggie wordlessly parted her legs.

"Good girl," he said. "But not yet."

They massaged her for ten minutes, their hands caressing her legs, her feet, her back, and the side of her breasts. Finally, when Maggie was almost ready to scream in frustration, they transferred their attention to her sex.

Ethan's hands slid over Maggie's ass, and he pulled her cheeks apart. "Hold them open for me, Maggie," he ordered.

Oh my God, the shame, Maggie thought. Her cheeks fiery, she did as he said. She felt hot oil drip down her crack, and then Ethan moved away. Out of the corner of her eye, she saw him get a butt plug from a wooden dresser. A big butt plug. "What are you doing?" she asked nervously.

"You're going to take this plug up your ass, Maggie," Ethan replied calmly. "You asked for the two-masseuse service, and we always deliver."

Was it too late to change her mind? She had thought they'd stick a finger up her butt, not a huge bulb-shaped *thing*. Before she could say anything, Lars shifted his focus to her pussy. His hands glided up her thighs, and his fingers spread her pussy lips. A sharp spike of desire jolted through Maggie, and she clamped her legs shut.

"If you don't keep your legs open for me, Maggie," Lars said, "I will tie your ankles to the legs of this table. You decide."

Raw, naked lust gripped her at the command in his voice. *Oh my God,* Maggie thought, her heart racing. *Who knew I'd be turned on with them barking orders at me this way?*

"Look at how wet she is, Ethan." Lars pushed a finger inside her pussy, and Maggie whimpered as he twisted the digit inside, seeking her g-spot. When he found it, his fingers curved and he pressed down on it, hard.

Maggie couldn't stop the moan that escaped her lips. "You like that, Maggie?" Lars asked, his mouth curving into a cocky grin.

Cocky grin or not, the man knew what he was doing. He added another finger, and her muscles clenched around him. With his other hand, he stroked her clitoris, tracing small circles around the engorged nub.

A finger caressed Maggie's anus, gently rubbing oil into her puckered asshole. "I'm going to enjoy this, Maggie," Ethan said, his voice deep with pleasure, as he pushed the tip of his finger into her tightly clenched hole.

She shivered with mingled fear and anticipation. "I'm sure you will," she said, her voice muffled by the towel that served as a pillow. "But will I?"

He spanked her ass in reply. "We haven't had any complaints," he said with a chuckle. He added a second finger to the first, and pushed in slowly, spreading the oil inside her channel.

Lars pulled his fingers out of her pussy, then thrust back in. "If you take that plug like a good girl, Maggie," he muttered, "I'll let you come." His thumb rubbed her clitoris, slow and steady.

Ethan removed his fingers from her ass, and then Maggie felt a cool weight at her asshole. It was the butt plug. She forced herself to relax as he pushed it in, slow but relentless. It stretched her wide, and she was about to whimper in discomfort when it popped into place.

It felt so weird. It filled her completely, and Maggie was very aware of the plug. It was so wicked, so naughty.

True to his word, Lars stroked her clitoris, pushing his fingers in and out of her slick channel. Maggie's orgasm started to build. Her muscles quivered, and the heat inside her boiled over. Then she couldn't hold back anymore. She bucked wildly on the table, her nails digging into the vinyl, and she came with a scream of pleasure.

"Would you like to schedule a follow-up appointment?" Lars asked when she had dressed again.

"Yes, please. Something for next week?"

They settled on a date, and he made a note of it. "Would you like the two-masseuse service again?" he asked her politely.

The butt plug was still in her ass. Maggie could feel it move with every step she took, and it was driving her crazy. She'd never been so turned on in her life.

"No." She looked at the two men. "This time, why don't you surprise me?"

I'VE BEEN TOUCHING myself as I write. My pussy is slick with my juices. As I write about Ethan and Lars, I can picture them touching me, pinching my nipples and smacking my ass. Taking me with forceful thrusts, making me erupt with pleasure.

"Fuck," I moan as my body tightens. The muscles in my pussy quiver and clench, and I come so hard that I see stars.

I don't know if my smut writing is satisfying a creative itch, but it's certainly doing wonders for my orgasm count. Of course, I'm failing at Life Rule Number 3. I'm definitely lusting after the jerks.

5

ETHAN

A week goes by. Catalina keeps calling, but much to Lars' relief, I start ignoring her calls. "It's about fucking time," he says when he sees me swipe my ex-wife's call to voicemail. "What brought on this change of heart?"

Perhaps it's because I've been masturbating to the thought of Maggie Zhang. At night, when I lie in my bed, I close my eyes and think dirty, filthy thoughts about our neighbor. I picture bending her over the foot of my bed and sliding my cock into her tight little pussy. I dream about wrapping my fingers around her long hair and tugging on it, and I fantasize about those pretty pink lips wrapped around my shaft as she struggles to take my length all the way down her throat. I imagine sucking on the pert nipples that had been so clearly visible underneath her shirt.

Since I'm not about to tell Lars any of that, I shrug with a show of indifference. "It was time."

Lars gives me a thoughtful look. "Good," is all he says. "In other news, the mayor of New Summit, a guy called

Richard Wagner knocked on our door today to welcome us to the town and invite us to the next downtown business association meeting. It's being held Thursday afternoon."

"You're interested in going?" Color me surprised.

"Don't sound quite so shocked," he replies. "I do my civic duty. Besides, after the towing episode, I've decided that it might be a good idea to play nice."

My lips twitch. "You could apologize to Maggie," I suggest slyly. "For yelling at her."

"Are you kidding me? She was going to get my car towed."

"You ignored her note."

"Yes," Lars says with exaggerated patience, "I did. Her note was full of snark, and I decided to take the high road. Rather than rub her nose in the fact that I did indeed have permission to park in her spot, I thought I'd let her figure it out on her own."

I snort. "Or you were too busy signing Cara Sandoval-Nez that you forgot all about it."

He grins unexpectedly. "Busted," he says cheerfully. "For the record, I did try to apologize a day after the towing incident, but there was a long line at the counter, and some guy was yelling that his order wasn't right. Maggie looked pretty stressed, and I didn't think my presence was going to be an improvement."

Yeah, I can't say I disagree with his assessment of the situation.

"Talking about Ms. Sandoval-Nez," Lars continues, "I think we should have a party to celebrate her signing. Invite a bunch of industry people, cocktails, finger food, blah blah, blah, the works."

We've assembled ReadSteam's core team. Katherine

Grant, who was the CFO of our old company, has signed on again as the new CFO. Natalie Knight, who's been our assistant for many years, is likewise happy to get to work again. Our third and fourth hires are Renee Smith and Carl Ramirez. Renee has a ton of New York publishing experience, and Carl is a marketing genius.

"Knowing Renee, she's going to invite every agent in Manhattan," I say dryly. As the editorial director, Renee's in charge of finding great books that will flourish in the ReadStream model, and she's wasting no time in charging ahead.

"Of course. I thought she'd want to do it in Manhattan, but she wanted us to host it here."

"Really? Why?"

"She thinks the building renovation is stunning, and I agree with her. You did a great job, Ethan. I have to admit that when I saw the shape the property was in when you bought it last year, I thought you were crazy to buy it."

My dad was an architect; I have a soft spot for old buildings. The renovations on the hundred-and-fifty-year-old building I bought on impulse have taken longer to complete than I'd anticipated, but the results are worth the wait. The four-story structure, a stunning example of Italian Romanesque Revival architecture, has been restored to its former glory, and the main floor, with its massive arched windows, will make a great venue for a party.

"Let's do it," I agree. "Natalie can set it up. How about Saturday, two weeks out?"

Lars checks our calendars and nods. "That'll work. I'll email Nat." He grimaces. "She's going to have quite a fun time trying to find a caterer in this town. So far, I've eaten bar food and generic Chinese. I never actually thought I'd miss Manhattan."

"You can be an elitist dick sometimes," I tell my friend. "There's nothing wrong with the Chinese food."

His eyebrows lift slightly, and his lips twitch, but if he has a comment to make about my quick defense of Maggie's restaurant, he doesn't say anything.

6

LARS

I'm not an elitist dick. It's not the Michelin star restaurants in Manhattan I miss; it's the shawarma stall that's down the street from my old condo.

Ethan knows that, which means his prickliness is about something else. Or someone else. Like Maggie Zhang. I have a sneaking suspicion that my friend likes our hot-headed neighbor.

The real reason I haven't headed over to the restaurant to apologize? I'm attracted to Maggie, and I'm not sure that I'll be able to resist asking her out. I have no desire to get in the way of my best friend. Ethan and I have been friends since high school. We founded our first company together; we worked long hours to make it successful, and through it all, nothing has ever come between us. Even Catalina.

I won't let Maggie Zhang be that person.

We turn the party planning over to Natalie. "There's not enough time for me to test a caterer in New Summit," she says to us when we talk to her on the phone. "So we're going to have to use Genevieve's crew."

"You're the expert," I reply and leave her to it.

ON THURSDAY, we show up to the local business association meeting, which is taking place in the coffee shop just down the street from us. Becky, who works there on weekends, gives us a wide smile when we come in. "Hey, you two," she greets us cordially. "How's life in New Summit so far?"

"Eventful," I reply dryly, thinking once again of Maggie Zhang. If she brings the same passion to bed, she'll be a fire-cracker. For an instant, I allow myself to imagine what that'll feel like, and I shake my head to clear my mind of those distracting thoughts. *Ethan likes her, dickwad,* I scold myself. *Stop driving yourself insane.*

"Really?" Becky's eyebrows rise. "You find New Summit eventful? Your life, before you moved here, must have been *incredibly* boring."

My lips twitch. I like the outspoken Hispanic woman. "Richard Wagner told us the business association meeting was going to be held here."

"It is." She points to a long table in the back, where about a half-dozen people are already seated. "Head on over. I've set out some coffee and cookies for us. It's a running New Summit joke that the mayor's never on time, but if you're lucky, he's only going to be fifteen minutes late."

Ethan laughs. "We'll keep that in mind for next time."

We walk over and greet the people who've already arrived. For some reason, all the older people sit on one side of the long wooden table, and the younger people sit on the other side. Maybe it's some strange small town custom.

Team Old consists of Pauline Fischer, who runs the grocery store, Debbie Marshall, who owns the under-whelming deli and Dr. Bollington, who stuffily informs us that he's a therapist as well as the landlord of this building.

Mrs. Ward runs a bed-and-breakfast, and Mr. Murray runs the downtown barbershop.

There are six people on Team Young. Cassie, who owns this coffee shop, is the only person we know. The others introduce themselves with friendly smiles. Mia Gardner owns the clothing boutique next door, and Nina Templeton runs the bar down the corner. Then there's Dr. Benjamin Young, who's a therapist as well, and Scott Leyland, who runs a concert venue next door. "Aren't you the lead guitarist of Evolving Whistle?" Ethan asks as soon the name registers. "I'm a big fan."

Ethan has a photographic memory, and it serves him well. Scott looks flattered, and Nina beams widely. "Everyone's talking about the restoration of the Morris-Stanton," she says, leaning forward. "For a while, it looked like the owner was going to demolish the building. I'm so glad you were able to save it."

Dr. Bollington frowns. "It should have been torn down," he says. "The place was an eyesore. Waste of money."

This is going to be good. If there's anything that winds Ethan up, it's the suggestion that old buildings be torn down to make way for modern construction. I'm still surprised he didn't become an architect himself. "Well," Ethan replies coolly, "it's a good thing I have an obscene amount of it."

Of course, that's when Maggie and her brother Dominic join us. Murphy's Law is a bitch.

THE TWO OF them sit down at the far end of the table. Maggie ignores us, but Dominic stretches forward to shake our hands. "Sorry about the parking mess-up," he says ruefully. "I forgot to tell Mags about it."

A wicked urge fills me. "No worries," I tell him.

"Matthew Steadman is done building the garage. The cars will arrive this weekend. Come over anytime you want a tour." I give Maggie a sidelong glance. Her hair's back in its usual ponytail, and the clothing she's wearing, a shapeless green dress, hides her soft curves. It doesn't matter. If I close my eyes, I can picture her yelling at me about my car, completely unaware that I can see the outline of her nipples clearly under her shirt. "You can take the Aventador out for a spin."

Ethan coughs pointedly. Yeah, I'm sure he's going to have something to say when we're alone. Heck, I haven't even let him drive the Aventador.

The kid's eyes gleam with excitement. "Really?" he asks. "That would be amazing."

Maggie gives me a cool glance. "You don't seem as concerned about your car today, Mr. Johansen. Last week, you seemed quite obsessed with your paint job."

Ethan shakes his head at me in warning, but something about this woman gets under my skin. I give her my most pleasant smile. "Well, I do have the license to do whatever I want," I say mildly, echoing the words she'd tossed at me last week.

Her eyes flash fire at me. "Of course you do," she says, through gritted teeth.

Just then, the mayor shows up. "Sorry I'm late," he huffs, sinking into his chair at the head of the table and reaching for the plate of treats in front of him. "Let's get going, shall we?" He bites into a chocolate chip cookie. "First, I want to thank everyone here for their help in getting our town ready for Pedestrian Saturday. The first event is this weekend, and I'm sure it'll be a great success."

Dr. Bollington doesn't look as certain as the mayor. "I think this whole idea is ridiculous, Bob," he grumbles. "All it's going to do is create a lot of mess on the streets, and make clean-up twice as expensive."

"Now, now, George," Richard Wagner chides. "Let's be realistic. New Summit's economy is propped up by tourism, and tourists like these types of events."

Cassie nods vigorously. "I totally agree," she says. "In fact, Maggie had an amazing idea for another event."

Maggie's cheeks turn pink. "I thought it would be fun to organize a night market."

Bollington frowns. "An event at night?" he says. "I don't like it."

Wagner's reaction is slightly more encouraging. "I'm not familiar with night markets," he says. "What are they?"

"They're street food festivals," Maggie says. "I thought we'd have multiple ethnic food stalls. Chase Henderson could showcase his new line of cider, and the Merry Cockatoo could offer samples of local craft beer in beer tents."

Pauline Fischer wrinkles her nose in distaste. "I don't like the idea, Richard," she says to the mayor. "Foreign food stalls? Beer tents? There's enough debauchery in our town already."

Maggie looks crestfallen, especially when the older woman says 'foreign food' in her snide tone. My temper rises. Mrs. Fischer is fucking oblivious. She's just insulted Maggie's restaurant, and she doesn't even realize it.

"I think a night market is a fantastic idea," I say quietly, keeping the irritation out of my voice. "Apart from the obvious impact on the restaurants in town, it'll also boost overnight stays."

An expression of surprise flits over Maggie's face.

Mrs. Ward, the owner of the bed-and-breakfast, has a calculating look in her eyes. "Maybe we're being too hasty, Richard? After all, we can't deny that New Summit is changing. There's new people in town, new construction. We should move with the times."

It's no wonder I'm cynical. Before Mrs. Ward realized that Maggie's idea was good for her bottom line, she'd been nodding in support of Mrs. Fischer. But with money on the line, her tune's changed.

The mayor looks doubtful. "I don't want to encourage public drunkenness," he says. "Beer tents…" His voice trails off, and he appears lost in thought, then his face brightens. "Tell you what," he says. "Why don't the two of you," he points to Maggie and me, "do some research on this issue? I'm sure other towns have held similar events. If you get me some estimates on what kind of security we need, then I'll work with Joe Laramie to set it up."

Maggie's mouth falls open. "Work with Mr. Johansen?"

"Of course." Richard Wagner is oblivious to the tension in the room. "That's not going to be a problem, is it?"

I don't bother concealing the smirk on my face. "I'd love to work with Maggie."

"Excellent." The mayor rubs his hands together. "Why don't the two of you report back at our next meeting? That's in four weeks. That should give you enough time, right?"

Maggie is glaring daggers at me. My grin widens. "Absolutely. Maggie, we're both busy this weekend. Why don't we meet Tuesday evening to discuss our plan of action?"

7

MAGGIE

Stupid, arrogant billionaires. Both of them. First, there's Ethan Burke, who announces that he has an obscene amount of money, then there's Lars Johansen, with his stupid smirks, deliberately baiting me by offering to let Dominic drive his pointlessly expensive sports car.

I've been writing dirty stories about them for the last week and a half, and I've been jilling off to images of Lars and Ethan doing wickedly filthy things to my body. Over the weekend, in a fit of boredom, I uploaded them to a site called Dirty Words, and now, I even have fans who comment on my work. The attention is both flattering and disconcerting, but thankfully, since I uploaded the stories anonymously, no one knows who I am.

"I like them," Dominic announces, reading my thoughts perfectly. "They seem like nice guys."

I snort. "You're just saying that because Lars offered up his Lamborghini as a bribe."

Dominic laughs. "He was just doing it to annoy you," he says astutely.

"It worked." My tone is sour. Lars Johansen also defended my night-market idea in front of everyone, and now the two of us are working together. Lovely.

"Are you okay, Mags?" My brother gives me a concerned look out of the corner of his eye. "You're not letting Lilly's news get to you, are you?"

Dominic might just be twenty-one, but he's perceptive beyond his years. I sigh. "I thought I wasn't," I admit. "Now, I'm not sure."

We walk in silence for a little bit. By unspoken agreement, we detour through the park. "Mom's been nagging me lately," Dominic says at last. "She wants me to go back to college. She thinks that she can manage the restaurant with your help."

"You know we can." My voice is gentle. China Garden doesn't need three people to run it. Dominic and I came back home when my father died, but it's been three years. Even my mom's moved on. She's started dating Patrick Fowler; she just bought a house on the outskirts of town, in a brand new subdivision. There's no need for Dominic to put his life on hold anymore.

What about you, Maggie? You're doing the same thing.

My brother clears his throat. "That's the thing, Mags. I don't want to go back to school."

I stop walking. "You don't?"

He shakes his head, a bitter twist to his lips. It's an odd look for my normally optimistic, happy-go-lucky brother. "Mom and dad wanted me to be a doctor or a lawyer," he says. "All I wanted to do was run China Garden."

"You do?"

"Yeah." He puts his hands in his pockets. "I don't want to be like Lilly or you, cooking at Michelin-starred restaurants, and I don't want to go to law school." He stares into the distance. "I like my life exactly the way it is."

I put my arm around my kid brother. "Have you told mom?"

"And break her heart?" He grimaces. "I'm working up the nerve to do it, Mags, but it's not easy."

"She loves you," I say, trying to reassure him. "She's going to want you to be happy."

"If that's true, why do we never mention Lilly to mom?"

I sigh. I wish I had an answer for him, but I don't. My mother was grief-stricken when she cut Lilly out of her life, and there's a deep vein of stubbornness in Angela Zhang. One Lilly and I have inherited, if I'm being honest. "We'll work it out. I'm on your side."

He hesitates before he asks the next question. "Do you want to run China Garden, Maggie? Am I making things difficult for you?"

"No." The only emotion I feel when I hear that Dominic wants to run the family restaurant is relief. I don't know what I'm going to do with my life once my brother gathers up the courage to tell our mother, but I'll figure it out.

ETHAN

"What the heck do you think you're doing?" I'm not sure if I should be angry with Lars or amused by the bemused expression on his face.

"I don't know," Lars admits. "I was sitting there, and that old bat said 'foreign food' with that look on her face, and I lost it a little."

"Oh, that's not what I'm talking about." If Lars hadn't jumped in to support Maggie's idea, I would have. "You offered to let Dominic Zhang drive your car."

"Ah." His lips twitch. "I admit, I was just doing that to annoy Maggie."

I snort. "Buddy, if you like the woman, ask her out. Don't do the equivalent of pulling at her pigtails, okay? We're not in grade school anymore."

Lars' expression shutters. "I don't like her that way," he says, his voice cool. "Shall we get to work? I don't know if you've noticed, but we're trying to launch a company here."

He's lying to me. I just don't know why.

MAGGIE

"*Dirty Words.* Explain."

It's the Tuesday after the first Pedestrian Sunday. Nina, Cassie, Mia, Becky, and I are in the Merry Cockatoo, eating lunch. Well, I'm eating lunch. The rest of them are just staring at me.

My newest life rule? If you're going to write smutty porn about your neighbors, don't get caught.

Here's what happened. Nina went to my apartment to take a nap over the weekend, and she saw my computer screen. Unfortunately, my browser had been open to the Dirty Words author portal, where I'd just finished uploading a story I'd written—*Ethan and Lars do the Cheerleaders.*

Now, I have some explaining to do.

"There's nothing to explain," I murmur, my cheeks fiery.

"I read your stories," Becky says. "They're very *explicit.*" Her lips curl into a grin. "Somebody has a crush on her neighbors."

"I do not," I respond indignantly. Becky's an artist who works in Cassie's coffee shop during the weekend. She paints lush close-ups of flowers, sensual and erotic, her work heavily inspired by Georgia O'Keefe. She's hardly one to talk about *explicit.* "I was looking for a creative outlet, that's all. It was Ben's idea."

Mia's mouth falls open. She carefully sets her pint of beer down on the table and gapes at me. "My Ben?"

Cassie's trying not to laugh. "Let me see if I've got this right," she says. "Ben West told you to write smutty stories about your hot neighbors. Uptight, buttoned-up, Dr. Benjamin West."

"Hey," Mia protests. "He's not *that* uptight."

"Okay, that wasn't exactly what Ben said," I concede. "He just told me to do something creative. He suggested painting, but I'm not artistic. So I thought I'd write a story."

"And you're not attracted to them?" Nina asks, her green eyes sparkling with curiosity. "Because I watched the three of you last week at the coffee shop. Sparks were everywhere."

"Those were sparks of hatred."

"Well, you know what they say," Becky says slyly. "The other side of hate is love..."

"Will you guys knock it off? First, I think they're stuck-up, entitled pricks. And second, just because most of you are in ménages, that doesn't mean I want one. Can you imagine my mother's reaction? No thanks. Life Rule Number 69: Maggie Zhang does not participate in threesomes."

"Do you actually have a list of these life rules?" Nina teases. "Or do you make them up as you go along?"

"She's making it up," Cassie giggles. "If you don't want a ménage, Maggie, then why are your smutty fantasies about both of them?"

I don't have an answer to her question, so I don't reply.

"And you're working with Lars on the night market

event?" Mia grins. "I can see how this is going to do down already."

Becky leans forward, her gaze avid. "You're meeting him today, aren't you? When?"

"At ten," I reply gloomily. "I'm cooking the dinner shift, and I head over as soon as I'm done. I wanted to move it to a different day, but Lars' schedule is complicated."

Cassie smirks. "You're going to be there late at night. They'll offer you a drink, and you'll accept because you don't want to be rude. The wine will relax you, and then..."

Nina's eyes dance with amusement. "Bow-chicka-wow-wow."

I get to my feet. Undeterred, they keep giggling. "Don't forget you have to tell us all about it," Mia says.

"Better yet, write a smutty story about it," Becky laughs. "And we'll all read it. Incidentally, Maggie, I found a typo in your *Lars and Ethan's Erotic Massages* story. Should I email it to you?"

I give her the middle finger. "Ladies, see you next week," I say with dignity. Their screams of laughter follow me out, and I have to bite my lips to keep from grinning widely. Nothing like a good session with my girls to cheer me up.

ON TUESDAYS, the restaurant closes at nine thirty. It's quarter to ten by the time I'm done cleaning the kitchen, and I just have enough time for a quick shower before I'm due next door.

I knock on the ornately carved wooden door, more nervous than I expected to be. My dirty stories have my hormones on high-alert. Cassie's question echoes in my ears. *If you don't want a ménage, why are your smutty fantasies about both of them?*

That's just your imagination at work, Maggie, I tell myself sternly, ignoring the way my pulse races. *In real life, they're a pair of dicks.*

Ethan opens the door, and my throat goes dry. He's shirtless, and his hair is damp as if he too just got out of the shower. I take in the tightly corded muscles, the smattering of hair that narrows down his flat stomach, the drops of water beaded on his chest, and I forget my greeting.

He's more self-possessed than I am. Of course. I've seen the pictures of his supermodel ex-wife, Catalina. Why on Earth would a man want meatloaf when he could have steak? "Hello Maggie," he says. "Come on in."

I enter the mostly-empty space. It's unfurnished except for a long table and an assortment of Aeron chairs. "You don't have any furniture," I exclaim. The main floor of the Morris-Stanton building is two thousand square feet, with large arched windows and high ceilings.

"No, not yet. I'm still trying to figure out what I'm going to do in this space." He smiles ruefully. "In Manhattan, my condo was six hundred square feet. When I moved here, I was sure I wanted a ton of space, but now that I have it..." He shrugs. "I'll figure it out."

"There are four floors, right?"

"Yeah, want a tour?" he asks casually. "Lars is on the phone, dealing with a last-minute work emergency."

"I'd love one." The Morris-Stanton has been an eyesore for years. When we were sixteen, a group of us had sneaked in through a broken window to explore the abandoned former hotel, and even though I'm not a history buff, my heart had broken at the obvious signs of neglect.

"Give me a minute to put a shirt on."

Bummer.

He shows me around the space, obviously proud at the

restoration. "The second floor will house ReadStream's offices," he explains. "Eventually. For the moment, we're still operating with a skeleton crew."

"Is ReadStream your new secret venture?"

He raises an eyebrow at me, and I blush. "The Internet was filled with speculation."

He chuckles. "No doubt. Well, it won't be a secret for long; we're holding a launch party on Saturday."

We climb two more flights of stairs. "Lars lives on the third floor," he explains. "I live on the fourth, and we both have access to the rooftop pool."

Whoa. "You have a pool?" Ethan and Lars both have a boatload of money. I shouldn't really be surprised.

"It's heated." His eyes rake my body slowly, *thoroughly*. I should feel outraged at the way he's looking at me, but I don't. My body heats, my insides quiver. "Feel free to use it anytime."

Calm down, Mags. He's just being neighborly.

"That's very kind of you." My voice is high-pitched and breathless.

"Kind isn't the word I'd use," he says under his breath. He opens the door to his apartment and ushers me inside. "The open concept loft apartment is something of a cliché," he says, his lips twisting into a grin, "but I couldn't resist. Can I get you a drink? I have wine, beer, and whiskey."

You're going to be there late at night. They'll offer you a drink, and you'll accept because you don't want to be rude. The wine will relax you, and then...

Bow-chicka-wow-wow.

But that's all just in my imagination. Ethan is just being polite. "Wine sounds good," I reply. "Thank you."

10

LARS

When I walk into Ethan's living room, the two of them are seated on the couch, laughing about something. Maggie's got her legs tucked up under her, and she's sipping wine, obviously relaxed and at home.

The moment she sees me, she stiffens. "Mr. Johansen," she says coolly, "it's good to see you."

"You can call me Lars," I tell her. I'm not sure why I'm irritated. Sure, I'm attracted to Maggie, but I'm a grown-up. It's obvious that Ethan has the hots for her. I should be glad they're getting along.

"There's an open bottle of red on the counter," Ethan says. "Grab a glass. What was the emergency?"

I fill my glass and bring the bottle over, topping the two of them up. "Desiree Palmer had some concerns about her contract."

"Why couldn't Renee handle it?" Ethan asks, with a frown. "Surely this is what we hired her to do."

I glance at Maggie, who lifts her chin up. "Are you afraid

I'll leak your secrets to the media?" she snaps. "Don't worry; they're safe with me."

"Heaven help me from high-strung women," I bite back. "I didn't want to bore you with shop talk, and I was wondering if you'd eaten dinner. You just finished a shift, didn't you?"

"Oh." She looks sheepish. "No, I didn't have time. I'll make myself something when I get back home."

"No need, I have food downstairs." I take a deep breath. If Ethan's interested in her, I need to make nice. I couldn't stand Catalina, and that didn't end well. I don't want to repeat old mistakes. "I'm sorry we got off on the wrong foot. I shouldn't have yelled at you about my car. I acted like a jerk. Can we call a truce?"

She curls a strand of hair around her fingers. "I did my share of yelling," she admits. "I'm sorry too." She sticks out her hand, and I shake it. She's a chef, and her hands are callused, but her skin feels warm, and her grip is firm.

Ethan rises to his feet. "You want a hand with dinner?" he asks me.

I shake my head. "It's just leftovers. It'll only take a couple of minutes to reheat. I'll get it."

11

MAGGIE

Okay, they might not be total jerks.

We eat dinner. When Lars said leftovers, I assumed I was going to eat some kind of takeout, but I'm wrong. The lamb *tagine* is obviously homemade, and it's delicious, an aromatic stew with chickpeas and apricots.

"You cook?"

Lars' lips twist into a grin. "You don't have to sound quite so surprised," he says. "I'm an adult in his thirties. Is it really such a shock that I can cook?"

The wine diffuses through me, loosening my tongue. "Well, yes." I wave airily, my attitude fueled by the Shiraz. "You're a billionaire. I thought you'd have staff for that."

They both roll their eyes. "We started our first company in a garage, Maggie," Ethan says. "Trust me; there was no staff. Either we learned to fend for ourselves, or we ate pizza. Cold pizza got old really quickly."

I should keep quiet, but discretion has fled the room. I'm tipsy, and they can tell, but they're both smiling, and after a really long time, I'm having fun. With a start, I realize I haven't flirted with anyone in years. In San Francisco, all my energies went into work, and in New Summit, single men are an endangered species.

"I can see Ethan cooking," I concede. "Not Lars though."

Ethan chuckles, and Lars looks outraged. "Why don't you think I can cook?" he demands.

I'm not being fair; Lars clearly can hold his own in the kitchen. I'm eating the very delicious results. Still, it's fun to get a rise out of him. "You drive around in a fancy sports car," I reply, my lips twitching at his expression. "You're obviously the playboy type. How many Lamborghinis do you own anyway?"

I'm expecting him to get angry at my glib characterization, but to my surprise, he grins. "I'm the furthest thing from a playboy, Maggie," he says, dark amusement dancing in his eyes. "If we're tossing around glib characterizations, I'm a workaholic with a penchant for speed."

"You're ducking my question," I reply loftily. "How many cars, Lars?"

"A dozen," he replies.

My mouth falls open, and I take a deep sip of my wine. "You have a dozen Lamborghinis? You've got to be kidding me."

Ethan rolls his eyes. "Sadly, no. My buddy here never saw a Lambo he didn't want to buy. It's an expensive hobby."

"It's cheaper than getting married," Lars says snidely. "All my cars together cost less money than the divorce settlement."

Ethan's lips twitch. "Touché," he says, conceding the point. I give him a curious look, trying to figure out if Lars' comment has bothered him, but if it has, I can't tell. He refills my glass of wine, his eyes on me.

"Are you trying to get me drunk?" I ask him.

At that, he grins. "Trying, no. Succeeding, yes. Do you want some water?"

EVENTUALLY, we discuss the night market. Lars has already been in touch with a couple of nearby cities that have held similar events, and he's got some numbers for me. "You did all the work," I accuse him.

"My assistant did all the work," he corrects me. "She's a whiz at this kind of thing."

"Oh. Thank her on my behalf. She saved me a ton of running around. I wouldn't have known where to get started."

"No worries," Lars says easily. "So help me understand something about New Summit. Why does Mrs. Fischer think that a night market is going to lead to sin?"

"Oh, that." I feel my cheeks heat. Stupid ménage fantasies. "She's not talking about the night market. She doesn't approve of Mia, Cassie, and Nina's relationships, and she never loses an opportunity to vocalize her disapproval."

"What doesn't she approve of?" Ethan's expression is confused.

I can't look at them. Every single one of the dirty stories I've written about the two of them runs like a movie reel through my head. "They're in ménage relationships," I mutter, staring at my glass of wine. "Not with each other," I clarify. "But Mia's living with Ben, who you met at the meeting, and Landon, who wasn't there. Cassie's with James and Lucas, and Nina's with Scott and Zane. It's quite the topic of gossip; I'm surprised you haven't already heard about it."

"Ménage?" Lars asks. There's a wicked gleam in his eyes. "Really? And people think small towns are boring."

I laugh at that. "I used to live in San Francisco," I reply.

"In the city, everyone's usually too busy working for debauchery, as Mrs. Fischer put it. New Summit, is, in comparison, a hotbed of naughty sex."

Ethan's eyes rest on me thoughtfully. "How interesting," he says. I want him to elaborate on his comments, but unfortunately, he doesn't. "What were you doing in San Francisco?" he asks instead.

"Cooking," I reply. He waits for me to elaborate. "I grew up around food. I wanted to be a chef, and San Francisco was a great place to learn."

"I've spent a lot of time in the Bay area," Lars says. "Where did you work?"

I'm not sure why I'm telling them my story. Perhaps it's because of Lilly's promotion, perhaps it's because I'm feeling stuck. "I was a line cook at Koi for two years," I reply. "I spent a year in Shanghai Kitchen, and then I trained at Saison for six months."

Lars looks impressed. "Why did you come back?" he asks. "No offense, but Saison is a three-star Michelin restaurant. What did New Summit have to offer?"

"My dad died," I reply shortly. "My mother needed help running China Garden."

"Ah," he says. "I'm sorry." He pours me more wine, and we talk about other, lighter things.

BACK HOME, I give myself a stern talking-to. *Maggie, this is demented. It's one thing to write smutty stories about them; it's another thing entirely to be charmed by Ethan and Lars.*

Falling for them would be stupid. Seriously dumb. They're way, way out of my league, and though they might flirt along with me, I'd be a fool to think that anything's going to come of it.

I need a cold shower. No, I need to stop lusting after the two of them.

Then a brainwave hits me. The only reason I'm attracted to Ethan and Lars is because I'm writing filthy smut about them. If I'm trying to get un-attracted to them, I need to do the opposite thing.

And no, the opposite thing isn't to stop writing the smut. It's too late for half-measures. What I need to do is make them unattractive jerks in my story.

Unattractive jerks, with very, *very* small cocks.

I open my laptop and start typing.

12

ETHAN

Thursday morning, ReadStream has its first full team meeting. Katherine, Renee, Carl, and Natalie drive down to New Summit, and we get down to business. Renee's offered contracts to two additional authors. Carl's got a ton of really great ideas for enhanced reading experiences, and a couple of hours pass in animated discussion.

"How's the party planning coming?" I ask Natalie when we're almost done.

She consults her notes. "Really good. A crew will be in tomorrow to clean the place and set up the decorations. Genevieve will show up Saturday at noon. Most of her food will be prepared in advance, but she needs an oven. I told her that wasn't going to be a problem."

Katherine's looking out of the window. "Can we break for an early lunch?" she asks. "I skipped breakfast, and I'm starving. Is the Chinese place across the street any good?"

"Maggie's restaurant? The food's tasty, but the menu's pretty standard fare."

Both Katherine and Natalie exchange glances when I say

Maggie, and they start giggling uncontrollably. I give Lars a mystified look, but he looks as puzzled as I feel. "Umm, ladies?" I raise an eyebrow. "What's funny about Chinese food?"

"It's not the Chinese food," Katherine says, through peals of laughter. "It's the name *'Maggie'*."

I'm missing something here. "Do you know Maggie?"

"No." Natalie's face turns pink. "It's just..." Her voice trails off, and she gives Katherine a helpless look.

Katherine clears her throat. "Sometimes, for, umm, recreational purposes, I read dirty stories on the Internet."

"Okay," Lars says, a blank expression on his face. "That's nice. Why would I care what you do in your free time?"

Natalie giggles. "Oh, just show them, Kat," she says. "I hardly think we're going to shock Ethan and Lars." She turns to Renee and Carl. "Kat and I both read stories on a site called Dirty Words," she says. "Well, about two weeks ago, someone uploaded a story on it. The only reason it caught my eye was because the guys in it were called Ethan and Lars."

Katherine hands me her phone. "And the girl's name is Maggie. Natalie and I have been getting quite a kick from reading them." Her grin widens. "Especially yesterday's chapter."

I start reading the story they're talking about, and my body goes still.

"Seriously?" Lars shakes his head. "Someone on the Internet writes some smut, and you're giggling because we share their names?"

Not just names. This is us, and there's not the slightest doubt in my mind that Maggie's the author.

"Fine," Natalie pouts. "Ruin our fun. The author did it already anyway with the last entry."

"What do you mean?" Renee asks. "How can she ruin your fun?"

I get to that part of the story. My eyebrows rise, and my lips widen into a grin. *She gave us two-inch dicks.*

This is war. Sexy, dirty, filthy, anything-goes war.

ONCE THE MEETING'S OVER, I tell Lars to check out Maggie's erotic stories. As he reads, he whistles silently. "The girl next door has some wild fantasies, doesn't she?" he says with a grin.

"She does." I hesitate, wondering how to broach the subject. Both Lars and I have done plenty of crazy things in our lives. While the two of us have never shared a woman, I've had a threesome once in the past, and so has Lars. "We could make some of them come true."

He looks at me, his expression troubled. "I thought you liked this woman, Ethan. If we do this, you might get jealous. I don't want you to end up hating me."

I could never do that. Lars is my best friend, and the bond between us is rock solid. Catalina, who hated Lars with a passion, had tried to come between us. Though I was a pushover for my ex-wife, this was the one thing at which she'd failed. "That's not going to happen," I say steadily. "Of course, if it bothers you..." My voice trails off.

"You're sure about this?" His tone is intrigued.

I nod.

"Okay." He takes a deep breath. "Let's find out if Maggie's actually interested. "Do you have a plan?"

"I do."

13

MAGGIE

I'm watching TV Thursday night when a movement catches my eye. Lars is standing near his window, looking directly at my apartment.

I shrink back, hoping he hasn't seen me, but my attention isn't on the television anymore.

He's naked. His shoulders are broad, and his abs are chiseled perfection, but that's not what my eyes are drawn to.

Nope. My eyes are glued to his cock. He's erect, he's extremely large, and he's touching himself.

As I watch, his fingers close around the base of his cock, and he fists himself. His eyes seem to stare right at me as he strokes up and down his shaft.

I'm held to my seat, transfixed by the raw masculinity on display. As he pumps himself, his thumb rubs his fat, engorged head. My hand snakes down my panties, and I part my pussy lips, flicking my fingertips over my clitoris. Closing my eyes, I imagine Lars and Ethan watching me, their eyes hot with desire as I touch myself. Would they be content to watch, or would they insist on helping out?

My phone rings, and I almost jump out of the chair. I look around guiltily, my heart racing in my chest. I feel like I've been caught with my hand in the cookie jar.

I don't recognize the number, but I answer it.

"Hello, Maggie." Ethan's voice is silky smooth. "Enjoying the show?"

My eyes fly to the building across the street. He can't see me, can he? I'm hidden in the shadows, out of sight. How does he know I'm watching Lars masturbate?

"I beg your pardon?" I bluff.

Dark amusement coats his voice. "I can see you, Maggie," he says. "Your fingers stuffed down your pretty pink panties, your thighs spread wide, your eyes glued to Lars' window. It's one of the advantages of being on the fourth floor."

"So you're peeping into my window? Isn't that a little perverted?"

He chuckles. "More perverted than writing dirty stories about your neighbors?" he asks. "Stories in which both Lars and I are taking you at the same time?"

My heart stops beating. My throat goes dry. Somehow— I don't know how—they've found out.

"What are you going to do?" I whisper. I'm the biggest idiot in the world. I used their first names in my stories. Not just theirs. Mine too. Why on Earth was I such a fool, and can they sue me for my stupidity? They're extremely rich. If they want to, they can ruin my life.

"That's not the relevant question, Maggie," Ethan replies.

"What is?" My palms are damp with sweat, and my skin feels cold and clammy.

"If you want to find out," he says, "Knock on our front door in ten minutes."

I dress with shaking fingers, putting on the first thing that I find in my closet. Part of me wants to hide under my covers and pretend that they haven't found out about the smut.

The more adventurous part of me is curious. What is the relevant question, and why do I have to go over there to find out?

I knock on their front door, and Lars opens it. He's wearing a pair of faded jeans and nothing else. "Hello Maggie," he says, his eyes gleaming with laughter. "Come on in."

I step into the main floor. Ethan's sitting on a chair at the side, his face in shadows.

Two days ago, the space was almost empty. Now, there's a massage table in the center of the room. Candles are everywhere, illuminating the room with flickering light. I can smell the sweetness of jasmine in the air, and the heavy sensuality of musk.

This is the setting of my first story.

"Are you going to sue me?" I blurt out.

Lars seems genuinely shocked by the thought. "Sue you? Why on Earth would we be that dumb?"

Ethan rises to his feet. "Suing you would just attract a whole lot of tabloid attention," he explains calmly. "It would be a whole lot easier for you to take the stories down."

"Of course." I nod eagerly. They're being a lot more understanding about this than I would have predicted. I thought they'd be furious, but if they are, it's well hidden.

"Then there's the matter of restitution." Lars' lips curve into a smile.

"Restitution?" A thousand butterflies take flight in my stomach.

"Your stories, as entertaining as they are," Ethan says,

stalking toward me, "are somewhat inaccurate when it comes to certain key details."

Ah. They've read my most recent story. My cheeks heat; a shiver wracks my body.

"There are two things you can do, Maggie." Lars looks at me, intent and assessing. "You can agree to take the stories down and you can walk out of the front door, free and clear."

"Or?" I whisper through dry lips.

"Or," Ethan says, his dark eyes glistening, "You can live out some of your fantasies."

A heartbeat passes. Then another. I stand there, more tempted than I've ever been in my life. What's the harm? I ask myself. I've been sensible all my life. I've been the dutiful daughter. For three years, I've put my family's happiness and well-being ahead of mine.

Can I have one night, just for myself?

My silence is answer enough. Lars moves behind me, and he locks the door, the sound loud in the quiet room. "Take your clothes off, Maggie," he says. "Get on the massage table."

Oh. My. God.

14

LARS

The stories were a revelation.

I'd caught a tiny glimpse of the true Maggie, the version she kept hidden from the world, when she'd come over on Tuesday. Then Ethan shows me her fantasies, and I catch another glimpse, and I want her.

"Take off your clothes, Maggie."

She bites her lower lip, her white teeth indenting the pink flesh. She's clearly nervous, but there's also a spark of interest in her eyes.

I'm more than a little surprised that she's still here.

She's fully clothed. She's wearing an old pair of jeans and a plain black t-shirt, and her face is scrubbed free of makeup. She's not trying to be alluring, but when I look at her, standing there, her expression uncertain, I'm more than a little turned-on. Maggie Zhang has a wicked side, and I can't wait to see it.

"Maggie. Now."

"I was getting there," she retorts. She unbuttons her jeans and slides them down her hips, then whips her t-shirt over her head.

I swallow when her body comes into view. Her small breasts are high and pert. Her nipples are erect, poking through the black lace fabric of her bra. Her hips are lush, and her ass? People should write odes about that ass.

"Your underwear too, baby." Ethan's voice sounds hoarse, and he can't take his eyes off her. I don't blame him; neither can I.

Maggie's hands go behind her back, pushing her tits up. She unclasps her bra and slips it off. I take the lacy garment from her.

"My panties too?" There's a definite tremor in her voice.

My lips curl into a grin. "I believe you were naked in your story," I say, my voice silky. "We shouldn't deviate from the script."

She chuckles, her tension evaporating. "Fair enough," she murmurs. She slips out of the panties.

I can't wait to thrust into her sweet, tight, little pussy. I can't wait to fill her, to hear her soft, breathy moans, to feel her muscles milk me as I ram into her.

"Very nice." My voice is raspy with need. *Stick with the script, Lars.* "Get on the massage table."

"What kind of massage am I having?" she asks archly. Her hips sway as she walks to the table, and my cock hardens in desire.

Ethan chuckles. "It's the two-masseuse special. I thought you'd be quite familiar with it."

"The woman in my story got a real massage first." She sits on the edge of the table. Her cheeks are flushed with desire.

"You're constantly underestimating us, Maggie." I stalk toward her. "Lie down on the table," I order.

She starts to lie down on her back, and I shake my head.

"On your stomach, honey." I pat the folded towel that's on one end of the table. "Use this as a pillow."

She takes a deep breath and rolls over onto her stomach. I reach for the bottle of massage oil closest to me. Ethan does the same. Drizzling some of the liquid on the back of her thighs and her calves, I lean forward to touch her naked body for the first time.

My heart is pounding in my chest. Not since I was a teenager have I ever been so painfully aroused by a woman.

15

MAGGIE

I feel the massage oil trickle over my flesh. "I'm going to start on your legs, Maggie," Lars says, his tone deep and dark and amused. "Ethan will work on your upper half."

They're quoting my story verbatim. A blush creeps up my cheeks. It was bad enough that my friends knew about Dirty Words, about the filthy, erotic fantasies I have about Ethan and Lars. But when the objects of my smutty desires find out? So embarrassing.

I don't know why I'm going along with this. I'm curious; how far will they take this role-play? I'm also aroused, aching, caught in a trembling lust. I'm not capable of rational thought.

Lars' big warm palms slide up my thigh, and my breathing catches. My insides clench and twist. "Have you memorized all the lines in my story?" I ask, to cover up the intensity of my need. "I'm so glad I have such ardent fans."

"We're only following your script to a point." Ethan uses the entire flat of his hands to stroke my back, and I arch into his strong touch, my body prickling with heat. "I'm not going to start gentle, Maggie," he says, moving in front of me and tracing the outline of my lips with his thumb. His dark eyes bore into mine. "You've been a naughty girl. You're going to take it hard."

I almost combust with need. Right there. Right in that moment. When Ethan Burke looks at me, his eyes glittering with heat, and tells me I'm going to take it hard.

The two of them touch me everywhere. Ethan places his hands on mine, then strokes up my arms, over my shoulders and down my back. Lars picks up where Ethan leaves off, the pads of his fingers caressing the cheeks of my ass. He doesn't linger, instead, he transfers his attention to the back of my thighs, massaging my legs and my feet.

For a few minutes, there's silence in the air, interspersed by my soft sighs of pleasure. They weren't lying; I'm getting a real massage. My skin is slick with massage oil, and every muscle in my body is relaxed.

Except those in my pussy. Heat builds between my legs. As Ethan works on my back, his erection is clearly visible beneath his pants.

Definitely not two inches, ladies and gentlemen.

Not going to lie, I lick my lips. Even drool a little.

Ethan's fingertips glide over the sides of my breasts, and I shift restlessly. "What's the matter, Maggie?" he asks. "Can't wait for the next part of the story?"

There have been so many fantasies about Lars and Ethan. My mind isn't working; I can't remember what I wrote in my first story about them. "What's the next part?"

Lars rests his palms on my ass cheeks and moves his hands in opposite directions, and that jolts my memory. The butt plug is next. The large glass butt plug.

My heart skips a beat.

"Ah, I see you remembered." Lars' finger teases at my tight hole, and he drizzles massage oil down my crack.

My fingers clench at the vinyl covering of the massage table. *You could say no, Maggie. You could stop them, grab your clothes and run away.*

"First time?" Lars' tone is unexpectedly tender.

Life Rule Number 53: The anus is an 'out' hole. *What the heck am I doing?* I bury my face into the towel. "Yeah," I mutter, my voice muffled by the fabric.

He presses a soft kiss on each globe. "I'll take it slow, Maggie," he promises. "It'll be good. Trust me."

Trust him? Strangely, I do. I still think Lars Johansen is entirely too smug and self-assured for his own good, but when he tells me it'll be good, I *believe* him.

His finger circles my tight anus, spreading the oil over me. He presses down slowly, pushing his finger into me. "You okay?"

Ethan brushes my hair away, and his warm lips tickle the skin at the back of my neck. My toes curl in pleasure at his kiss, and I moan in response. Lars takes my moan as assent. He adds another finger, slowly stretching my puckered asshole. "You like this, Maggie?"

Strangely, yes. I've never had anal sex before. The act has always felt taboo. Wrong. Dirty. Wicked. "Yes," I whisper. "It's so intense."

My pussy is dripping. If either of them touches me, they'll discover the truth. I'm so turned on that I can't think, I can't focus, I can't even breathe.

While Lars carefully eases his fingers in and out of my asshole, preparing me for the butt plug, Ethan's fingers caress the side of my breasts. "Lift up," he instructs me.

I push myself up on my elbows, and his fingers find my nipples. He rolls the hard nubs between his thumb and forefinger, and I writhe on the table, my fingers gripping the sides as if my life depended on it.

Lars' fingers withdraw from my ass. I feel him move away. He's back in a minute, and he swings into view. "We went shopping this afternoon," he says, showing me the unopened box. "Ethan and I had to guess at what type of plug you wanted." His lips curl up. "I'm pretty sure you're going to enjoy this one."

I'm sure he's right, but he's a little too self-assured. "So cocky," I mock. "What if I hate it?"

He chuckles. "Maggie, you're soaked." He moves behind me, and his fingers trace the outline of my pussy lips. "You're so beautiful, baby. So wet, so ready for this. Hold yourself open for me."

What? I freeze. I can't do that. I can't spread my cheeks apart; I can't expose myself to Lars' hungry gaze.

He swats my ass. "Is there a problem?" he asks, his voice steely.

My insides twist with desire. *Oh God. That spank. That tone.* Lars obviously expects to be obeyed, and strangely, his dominance fills me with desperate trembling. Outside the bedroom, if he uses this tone on me, I will knee him in the groin, but when I'm naked and wet? *Bring it.*

With shaking fingers, I obey. "What a pretty little ass you have, Maggie," he says.

Ethan moves behind me as well. "Oh fuck," he breathes. His fingers grip my cheeks as well, spreading me wider.

I feel fresh oil trickle over me, and then the blunt tip of the butt plug is at my anus.

Instinctively, I clench. "Calm down," Lars says, his voice soothing. "I'm not going to go faster than you're ready for, Maggie."

"She needs a distraction." Ethan lets go of my butt. "Turn over, Maggie."

I comply with the instruction, closing my eyes, so I don't have to look at their faces. I'm so mortified at how wanton I'm being, but I can't bring myself to stop. *I want this.*

"Good girl," Ethan praises. He cups my breasts, bringing them together, and squeezes gently. He lowers his mouth to my nipples, sucking them, nibbling at them. His stubble scratches my delicate skin, and the sensation sends a sharp spike of heat through me. "Tell me what you like."

"I like this," I breathe. "Don't stop."

"I have no intention of stopping," he assures me.

Seeing that I'm distracted by Ethan's attentions, Lars oils up the plug again. This time, I force myself to stay focused on Ethan's kisses, the way his teeth nip at my engorged tips... My tight hole stretches as the plug invades my body, and I whimper in discomfort.

"Relax, Maggie," Lars says. He parts my folds with his finger and brushes a thumb over my clitoris. At the same time, his other hand holds the plug, exerting steady pressure.

And then it's in. My skin stretches to accommodate the fat bulb. Every nerve ending in my body comes alive. My insides are heavy with lust, and my pussy weeps with need.

"How does it feel?" Lars asks. His fingers trace the base of the plug, and I feel the movement deep in my core.

I'm full. Uncomfortably full. I'm very aware of the plug in my ass. I'm almost ready to explode. I don't care about my stupid story anymore; I want them with desperate need.

"Amazing," I whisper.

"Open your eyes, Maggie," Ethan says. "Don't hide from us."

My eyelids flutter open. Lars stares at me, his green eyes

inches from mine. "Hey there," he whispers, then his lips meet mine in a hungry, intoxicating kiss.

I can smell the clean male smell of him, soap mingled with man. I can see his biceps bulge as he holds himself over me. His fingers are slightly callused—*from working on his cars?*—and when he strokes my upper arms, goosebumps rise on my flesh. His tongue probes my mouth, exploring me thoroughly. I groan deep in my throat and kiss him back, almost mindless with need.

While Lars kisses me, Ethan moves between my legs. He bends my knees up, exposing my pussy to his gaze. "Very pretty," he mutters. Then his tongue swipes over my slit.

I stop breathing.

Lars' mouth sucks a nipple, pinching the other one between his finger and thumb. At the same time, Ethan rubs his hands up and down my legs. His stubble grazes my inner thigh, and he kisses me there, softly and tenderly.

I can't hold back my groan of need. "Please, Ethan," I beg.

"Please what, Maggie?" Ethan exhales on my exposed pussy, and I shiver in response. "Tell me what you want."

"Please..." I plead, my cheeks heating. To my everlasting gratitude, he doesn't make me say the mortifying words. He bends his head back to my pussy. His lips graze my folds, and he slides his tongue up my slit, a light, teasing stroke that sends pinpricks of lust radiating through my body.

I will die if he doesn't hurry up. They've massaged me. They've stroked every inch of my body. They've pushed a butt plug into my ass. If Ethan doesn't make me come now, I will lose my mind. "Stop teasing me," I pout, thrusting my hips into his face.

Lars chuckles. "Go slower," he advises his friend. "Maggie's under the delusion that she controls the pace."

Ethan laughs too, but he takes pity on me. He kisses my clitoris, and his tongue traces slick circles around my glistening, engorged bundle of nerves. I whimper and groan, my head thrashing from side to side. Lars works my breasts; Ethan eats me out. I'm so close.

My fingers dig into the vinyl tabletop, so tightly I'm afraid I'm going to tear it. Ethan pushes his finger into my pussy, twisting it inside until he finds my g-spot. My breathing catches as he presses down, adding another finger at the same time.

Lars nips my nipples, sharp bites that make my flesh throb. I twist and flail, trying to squirm away from the sensations that are threatening to overwhelm me, but neither of them let me flee. Ethan grips my hips and won't let me escape. His tongue is unrelenting, as are Lars' fingers.

My pussy aches. I tremble and quiver under their onslaught. I moan aloud. This feels so good; I can't hold back...

Then the dam bursts. My muscles tighten, and my body stiffens, and I explode, screaming as my climax shudders through me. Ethan doesn't stop licking my pussy; he continues his assault until I can't take it anymore.

I push him away, and I sit up, a wide grin on my face. Tomorrow morning, I'll worry about the consequences of giving in to my desire, but right now, I feel amazing. My skin feels flushed, and my body is sated. Ethan and Lars gave me an unbelievable amount of pleasure, and I want to reciprocate.

"That's where the story ends," Lars says, stepping away from me.

"Does it have to?" I ask softly.

They look at me searchingly. "I don't want to pressure you into anything, Maggie," Ethan says.

I roll my eyes. "I am capable of knowing what I want," I tell them.

Lars' lips twitch. "I never doubted it for a second," he replies solemnly. "You want to get fucked, Maggie?"

Yes. I've never wanted anything more.

ETHAN

My dick is so hard that it's painful. Tasting her, feeling the way her pussy milked my fingers, I need more.

"Get on your stomach," I order, and she obeys. I strip quickly, and she watches, her dark eyes heated. She makes no effort to conceal her desire. "Like what you see?" I ask her.

She nods. "Oh yes." Her mouth falls open as my cock springs into view.

Lars reaches for Maggie's arms, and he pulls her up. "Do you want to taste him, Maggie?" he asks. "He's not two inches, is he? Will you be able to take him in your mouth?"

She licks her lips, and I almost blow my load. "I'm certainly going to try," she says. She pokes her tongue out, flicking at my head. Then she opens wide and takes me in her mouth.

Fuck me. I've died and gone to heaven.

Her cheeks turn pink as she licks my shaft. She bobs forward and takes me as deep as she can, the muscles in her throat swallowing as she struggles to take my length.

"Just a second." Lars repositions her so that she's on her knees. He tears open a condom wrapper and gives her a questioning look. She nods enthusiastically. I wait as he rolls the condom on and pushes into her sweet pussy, but I don't need to prompt Maggie. As soon as Lars is sheathed in her, her hands reach for my cock. She pumps my length before taking me in her mouth again.

My head falls back, and a harsh groan escapes my lips. "Fuck yes," I moan, as her lips suck my head and her hand fondles my balls. At this rate, I'm not going to be able to hold off my climax. "Maggie, if you don't slow down, I'm going to come in your mouth," I warn her.

Her eyes are glazed with desire as Lars thrusts into her. She swirls her tongue around my head and wraps her pretty pink lips around my cock, and the sight of it is more than I can resist.

Each time Lars pumps into her, her head bobs forward on my shaft. Sex has never been so intense, so mind-consuming. I can't think. The scent of Maggie's arousal fills the air, and it's a powerful drug.

I wrap one hand in Maggie's hair, tugging her mouth deeper. My other hand strokes her cheek. "So good," I groan. "So fucking good, Maggie. You want to swallow, baby?"

"Yes," she breathes.

Lars rams into her, hard and uncontrolled, his face contorted with pleasure. His fingers work her pussy and I stroke her face, and then I can't hold back. I explode in her mouth, and she swallows every drop.

WE PAUSE for a little while to catch our breaths and recover. Maggie removes the butt plug, and we shower together, long and slow, cleaning off the massage oil. Then we go at it again.

I can't get enough of Maggie. "Stay the night," I tell her after the second round of lovemaking. It's late, almost two in the morning, and the three of us are on my bed.

She shakes her head. "I can't," she replies.

"Why not?"

She doesn't meet my eyes. "I have to work in the morning, Ethan."

"Have dinner with us sometime next week?" The next few days are going to be crazy with the party and the official launch of ReadStream. Our website goes live tomorrow, and Lars is working on a couple of major contracts. But I don't want to let Maggie go. I definitely want to see her again.

"Sure." She gets to her feet, and she smiles at the two of us. "I'll take the stories down," she says, her cheeks pink. "Thanks for not suing me."

Suing? We've just spent the last few hours making love to this woman, and she's thinking about litigation? I'm missing something.

Before I can probe, she's dressed. She gives us a brief hug and runs down the stairs. I watch her cross the street from my window, and then she's in her apartment.

THE NEXT DAY, I'm shopping in New Summit's only grocery store when my phone rings. It's our assistant Natalie. "I have some bad news," she says, her voice stressed. "Genevieve's father had a heart attack this morning. She's canceling on us. I've spent the last two hours calling every catering company in Manhattan, but no one can make it all the way to New Summit on such short notice. I've searched on the

Internet, but the town you live in doesn't appear to have any caterers. I tried to call Lars, but he's in Chicago for the day."

Natalie sounds like she's hyperventilating. "Calm down," I tell her. "It's just a party."

She takes a deep breath. "I've ordered a dozen cheese and charcuterie trays," she says. "But we're screwed for hot appetizers."

"Maybe not," I reply thoughtfully. "I might be able to find us a backup option."

MAGGIE'S POURING a couple some steaming hot tea when I walk into China Garden. When she sees me, she looks wary. "Hello Ethan," she says. "What can I do for you?"

I frown. "Did I do something wrong?" I ask bluntly.

"No, of course not," she replies. "Thank you for the flowers this morning. It was a nice gesture."

I could live to be a hundred years old, and I still won't understand women. "Maggie," I say patiently. "I like to think I'm smarter than the average guy, but maybe I'm fooling myself. You're not meeting my eyes, which tells me that I've screwed up somehow, *but I don't know what I did.* So help me out here."

My ex-wife Catalina would go off into a snit for no reason and refuse to tell me why. Her favorite line was 'If you don't know what you did, then I'm not going to tell you.' To my surprise, Maggie doesn't play games. "I'm just surprised to see you here," she says, looking slightly uncomfortable. "I thought last night was a one-night stand."

A one-night stand? Her assumption bothers me more than I expect. "Why would you think that? We invited you to dinner."

She rolls her eyes. "Your precise words were, 'Have

dinner with us sometime next week.' *Sometime* is guy code for *never*. You might as well have said, 'Don't call me, I'll call you.'"

For crying out loud. "My schedule this week is crazy. I don't know if you remember, but when I said that we should have dinner, I was naked. I didn't have my phone with me, and I couldn't look at my calendar."

"Oh." She still doesn't meet my gaze. "Is that why you're here?"

"No," I reply. I wonder if she's regretting last night, but I'm reluctant to ask. I don't want to hear the answer. "I definitely want to have dinner with you, but that's not why I came to find you. I need a favor. Lars and I are having our launch party tomorrow night, but our caterer has bailed on us. I was hoping you'd fill in."

17

MAGGIE

They want me to cater their fancy party. The real shocker? I want to do it. It's been three years since I've been enthusiastic about cooking, but when Ethan asks if I'd help them out, excitement fills me.

I'm supposed to be cooking at China Garden tomorrow, but Dominic will cover for me if I ask. "I'd love to," I reply. "How many people are you expecting, and what kind of food were you thinking?"

"One hundred and twenty-five people," he replies. "And I'll take anything. If you said no, my next option would have been pizza."

He grins when he says that, and my insides clench. This morning, I could hardly believe how wild and wanton I'd been last night, but when Ethan Burke smiles at me, I get it. Ethan is an irresistible combination of charm and sexiness.

"Okay." I smile back at him. "I might not be as good as your original caterer, but I'll definitely be better than pizza."

"You're a lifesaver, Maggie," he says, taking out his wallet. "Five hundred dollars sufficient for a deposit, or do you need more?"

"Are you kidding?" I look around the restaurant. My mother's nowhere in sight. Thank heavens. I lower my voice. "I slept with you. I'm not going to charge you. That's just weird."

Ethan's gaze is warm. "You have to buy groceries," he says patiently. "I'm incredibly grateful for your help, Maggie, but you don't need to work for free. We were paying Genevieve a thousand dollars for her travel time, and an additional seventy bucks per person for food. Will that work?"

I do the math in my head. "That's almost ten thousand dollars." Holy fucking shit, that's a lot of money. "Ethan, I'm not going to charge you ten thousand dollars, that's crazy. Tell you what. Reimburse me for groceries. I might have to hire Sophia and Becky to help me with prep, and if I do, you can pay them twenty-five dollars an hour. Okay?"

"Not okay," he replies. "But I'm not going to argue with you now. Do you need help with the groceries?"

I shake my head. "I've got this." Finger food for a hundred-plus people. It's spring. Fresh asparagus is every-where, so I'll make prosciutto-wrapped asparagus spears. Onion and goat cheese tartlets. Chorizo-filled dates wrapped in bacon. The ideas dance in my head, and my fingers itch. I can't wait to get started.

Screw the dirty stories. This is what I need.

18

MAGGIE

I spend most of Saturday preparing for the party, cooking in China Garden's kitchen, Dominic and me dancing around each other in an intricate shuffle. "So you're cooking for the billionaires, huh?" he asks. "You've decided they're nice guys after all?"

"Have you told mom you don't want to go back to college yet?" I quip back at him.

He laughs. "Nice try, Sis. Admit it, Lars and Ethan are good people. Have you seen Lars' Lamborghini collection yet?"

"No." *Because I've been too busy sleeping with them.* "Fine, they're not bad. Lars has been pretty helpful about the night market idea."

"That's good." Dominic rinses a couple of heads of bok choy in the stainless steel sink. "I know I have to tell mom," he says after a long pause. "I'm working up the nerve."

I can understand. Part of the reason I was so nervous around Ethan yesterday was because my mother was cooking in the kitchen, and I was afraid she'd come out and see the two of us talking, and that would lead to a lot of questions.

Mom's dating Patrick Fowler, and Patrick's son James and his friend Lucas are in a ménage with Cassie, but my mother's never talked about their relationship.

I can't tell her about Lars and Ethan. Last night was amazing. Probably the best night of my life. *But it needs to be a one-time thing.*

SLIGHTLY AFTER NOON, the door to the kitchen opens, and Patrick limps in. Dominic looks as surprised as I feel. Although Patrick and my mom have been dating seriously for almost three months, I've never seen him in the restaurant.

"Hey Patrick," Dominic greets him. "Are you looking for mom? She's not working here today."

He shakes his head. "I wanted to talk to the two of you," he says. "It's Angela's birthday in a month, and she let it slip last night that it's a milestone year."

"Yeah, she's going to be fifty-five," I confirm. "Mom hates celebrating her birthday though. She's weird about it."

Patrick grins. "Well, I talked her into letting me throw a party for the occasion. I came by to invite you, and check that I'm not interfering with any of your plans?"

We both shake our heads. When he's gone, Dominic turns to me. "Do you think Patrick knows about Lilly? Should we tell him?"

I'd talked to my twin yesterday. I'd told her all about Lars and Ethan, and she, in turn, had told me about a fellow chef that she's dating. Yet not once during the forty-five-minute conversation had she mentioned my mother. I can't see a reconciliation happening anytime soon. "I'm not getting in the middle of that mess," I tell my brother.

He sighs heavily, but he doesn't try to change my mind.

Sophia and Becky show up at four and help me load the food onto trays. "It's a good thing the party's across the street," Sophia says cheerfully. "If you're going to become a caterer, you need a van, Maggie."

She loads four trays on a cart and wheels it to Ethan and Lars' place. When she's gone, Becky turns to me. "So," she says. "The billionaires that you hate. Tell me again why you're catering their party?"

"Twenty-five dollars an hour."

"Really?" She sounds skeptical. "You met Lars Tuesday night to discuss the night market, didn't you? How was that?"

"It was fine," I mutter, my eyes on the tray of asparagus in front of me.

"And was there any bow-chicka-wow-wowing?"

My cheeks heat and Becky stares at me. "Oh my God," she says. "I was just teasing you, but something happened, didn't it? Tell me everything."

I look around nervously. Dominic's nowhere in sight. "Fine, we made out," I whisper. "But don't tell anyone, please. I don't want to make a big deal of it. It's not going to happen again."

"You made out with Lars?"

I glare at her. "Lower your voice, damn it. I don't want Dominic to hear." I take a deep breath. "It wasn't Lars," I confess. "It was both of them."

Her mouth falls open comically. "At the same time? Oh. My. Fucking. God. Tell me everything."

Life Rule Number 29: Don't kiss and tell. "Yeah," I mutter. "That's going to happen. Becky, can we drop this?"

"No way. You swore up and down on Tuesday that you weren't going to join the ménage wagon. What made you change your mind?"

A massage table. A dirty story. Two very hot men. "It doesn't matter," I insist. "It was a lapse in judgment. It's never going to happen again."

Her expression turns sympathetic. "Why not? Was the sex awful?"

"No," I say at once. "It was great."

"So," Becky says, giving me a confused look. "Why just the one time?" Her expression darkens. "Did Ethan and Lars blow you off?"

"No." I sigh. "I can't do what Mia and Cassie and Nina are doing, Becky. My mother lives in New Summit. If the town gossips about me, *and you know they will,* my mother's going to get hurt."

Becky doesn't look like she's done with our conversation, but she subsides when Sophia comes back to the restaurant, followed closely by Lars and Ethan. "I brought muscle," she announces cheerfully.

Becky starts coughing, and I kick her ankle under the table, glaring at her fiercely. If she doesn't cut it out, Ethan and Lars are going to figure out that I was talking about them. She takes pity on me, and she pastes a bland look on her face.

Lars grins at me. "That's right, ladies," he says lazily. "Put us to work. Maggie already knows that I can pull my own weight in the kitchen."

I blush. Maggie and Sophia are both giving me curious looks, and I know I'm in for an interrogation tomorrow. I take a deep breath. For the moment, I have to set that aside.

There's too much work to be done. "Just carry the food across the street," I tell them. "And I'm going to need to use both your ovens."

Sophia, Becky, and Ethan grab trays of food and cross the street. Lars hangs back. "Hey," he says softly, leaning toward me and brushing his lips across mine. "Thanks for doing this."

My skin prickles in response to his touch. "No worries," I whisper.

"How are you?" he asks. "Sorry I didn't call you yesterday. I was in meetings in Chicago."

"You don't have to explain. You don't owe me anything."

His eyes darken. "Maggie," he says, "We went over this Tuesday, remember? I'm not a playboy. My casual sex days are in the past." His fingers stroke my arm as he talks and goosebumps rise on my skin in response to his touch.

I swallow, hard.

"Ethan said there'd been some kind of mix-up over dinner," he continues. "We cleared our calendars tomorrow, and it's supposed to be a gorgeous day. Will you spend it with us? We can go somewhere if you'd like, or we can just laze around by the pool."

I should decline. But Lars is looking at me, his expression warm and sincere, his lips inches from mine, and I don't have the ability to resist. "Okay."

"Good." He kisses me again, quick and hard. Letting me go, he picks up an armful of Tupperware containers and makes a wry face at me. "Now, for the schmoozing."

I laugh at his sour face. "You're not looking forward to this evening?"

"I like hanging out with my friends," he replies. "This is work." He grins at me. "I am looking forward to the food."

We fall into a rhythm, Becky, Sophia, and I. Sophia

works in Nina's kitchen, and she's a good cook, so I let her deal with the more complicated dishes, while Becky minds the oven.

Before the party gets underway, a young woman walks into Lars' kitchen, which I've commandeered for the evening. "You must be Maggie," she says to me with a friendly smile. "I'm Natalie. Thank you so much for helping. I couldn't get angry with Genevieve for bailing on us, but I was freaking out when I called Ethan yesterday morning."

"No worries." I study Natalie covertly. She's wearing a beaded, jewel-green top and dark skinny jeans. Her dark hair hangs in large curls down her back. "You did all the research on night markets, didn't you? Thanks so much for that."

She grins. "Oh, I was happy to help out. I was thrilled when Lars and Ethan called, telling me they were starting another company. I was going out of my mind with boredom."

"You worked for them at their old company?"

She nods proudly. "Yup. I've worked with them for seven years. They're awesome." A loud crash sounds through the house, and she winces. "I better go see what that's about," she says. "If you need anything this evening, just find me."

LARS

The party's going great. Everyone oohs-and-aahs over the Morris-Stanton renovation. "Great office, Johansen," George Arnold, the CEO of a large New York publishing house says to me enviously. "You're probably paying a fraction of the rent we are for ten times the space."

"Ethan owns the building," I reply with a smirk. Most of the people in this room thought we were insane moving out of Manhattan, but I can tell that they're reconsidering.

Renee is surrounded by agents pitching her books. The food's a huge hit, and the bartenders can barely keep up with the demand.

Everything's going great until Ethan's ex-wife Catalina shows up.

Next to me, Natalie sucks in her breath. "What the fuck is she doing here?" she mutters. "She's not on the guest list."

I watch Catalina swoop up to Ethan, and lace her arm through his. Ethan, to his credit, looks furious and tries to pull away, but the supermodel clings to him like a limpet and doesn't let go.

"When has that ever stopped her before?" I ask bitterly. My thoughts are on Maggie. I don't want her to see Ethan arm-in-arm with his supermodel ex-wife. She'll get the wrong idea.

Marching up to the two of them, I pull Ethan aside. "What the fuck are you doing?" I demand, my voice low. "Maggie's in my kitchen. Do you want her to see you with your ex?" My protectiveness takes me by surprise.

Ethan looks alarmed. "Keep Maggie away," he says. "I'll do my best to get rid of Catalina, but you know what she's like. If I throw her out, she'll make a huge scene, and tomorrow morning, it'll be in the Post."

He's right. I don't want ReadStream's launch marred by Catalina's tantrum. "Fine," I reply. "I'll make sure Maggie doesn't find out, but Ethan? This shit with Catalina has got to end. You've got to make it clear to her that you're done. Either that or cancel dinner plans with Maggie. You can't have it both ways."

"I'm not trying to," he replies through gritted teeth.

That's unfair of me, I know. But I really don't want to expose Maggie to Ethan's manipulative ex-wife.

I VISIT Maggie in the kitchen as often as I can, but it's not until the end of the evening when I find her alone. "Hey," she greets me, looking up with a smile as I come in. "I was afraid we'd run out of food there," she says ruefully. "Everyone ate twice as much as I'd planned."

"The food was a huge hit," I tell her. "I thought a fight was going to break out over the scallop carpaccio."

She blushes. "Thank you," she says.

I look around. "Where is everyone?"

"Becky's upstairs, cleaning the mess we made of Ethan's kitchen," she says. "And I just sent Sophia home."

"Good." I wrap my hand around the back of her neck, and pull her toward me, breathing her in, feeling her softness against me. I nibble small kisses on her jaw and nip gently at her earlobe.

Maggie moans and throws her head back, and I transfer my attention to her neck. "What are you doing, Lars?" Her voice is breathless.

"Expressing my appreciation," I reply. "The party was a fantastic success, thanks to you." Except for Catalina's presence, but with any luck, Maggie'll never find out about her.

She smiles, her expression pleased. "You flatter me," she says. "I'm pretty sure the Lamborghini collection got much more attention than my food."

"Yeah." I scowl darkly at the memory of a hundred inebriated people stumbling around near my cars. "I almost couldn't watch the carnage."

She laughs softly. "I can imagine," she says. "The first time I met you, you went ballistic at the thought of your paint getting scratched."

"And you told me I was an entitled jerk."

"I didn't use those precise words," she protests.

I grin at her. "You didn't have to. Your opinion came through, loud and clear."

She stands on tiptoe and trails a kiss across my lips, one that instantly makes my cock rock hard with desire. "I've reconsidered my opinion," she whispers into my ear. "The two of you might not be so bad after all."

That's when the doors swing open and the wait staff wheels in a tray filled with dirty dishes.

And just outside, a dark-haired woman is locked in a passionate embrace with a man.

It's Catalina, and she's sticking her tongue down Ethan's throat.

I turn to Maggie, trying frantically to think of something to say that's going to smooth the moment over. But I've got nothing.

Her face is white. "You didn't need to lie to me," she says, her voice quiet and strained. "Neither of you." She laughs bitterly. "You know what, Lars? For a second, I almost believed the bullshit."

With shaking fingers, she rips her apron off and throws it on the counter. Then she pivots on her heels and leaves.

Fuck.

20

ETHAN

Fucking Catalina. All evening, she clings to me, and I keep quiet. We're surrounded by publishers, agents, and prospective clients, and I'm reluctant to make a scene.

But it's midnight, the party's winding down, and the room's emptying out. I don't have to pretend anymore.

Catalina comes back from the bar with two glasses of champagne in her hands. She hands me one. I take a deep breath and brace for a scene. "What are you doing here, Catalina?" I ask her bluntly.

She laughs gaily. "Why, Ethan, you sound like you don't want to see me," she says, tucking her arm into mine. "Is that any way to talk to your wife?"

"Ex-wife. You asked for a divorce. Don't you remember?"

She gives me a coy look through her eyelashes. "I made a mistake," she says. "Won't you forgive me for it?"

I open my mouth to reply, but before I can tell her it's over, she puts a finger over my lips. "Give me a tour of the place, Ethan?"

"Fine." It's probably better to have this conversation somewhere private. Catalina's not above making a scene if it'll get her what she wants.

I show her around. She's uninterested in ReadStream's offices on the second floor, but her eyes sharpen when she surveys Lars' apartment. "You were always very close," she murmurs. "And now, you live together."

She starts walking around the open-concept space, and I frown. "You can't walk into his apartment, for fuck's sake," I snap.

She rolls her eyes. "You're so uptight, Ethan," she chides. "Where's your sense of fun?" She pushes me against the wall. "I've missed you," she pouts. "Don't you miss me?"

And saying that, she kisses me.

For a second, my mind goes blank with shock. Just for a second. Then I remember Maggie, and I push her away.

But it's too late; the damage has been done. When I lift my head, I see a white-faced Maggie staring at me, then she pushes past both Lars and me, running down the stairs.

"What the fuck have you done?" Lars snarls as he takes off in pursuit of her.

I've fucked up. I need to do what Lars is doing, follow Maggie home and try to explain what she saw wasn't real. But first, I need to deal with Catalina. I've been passive about this situation too long.

"Listen to me," I say, my voice a barely suppressed snarl of rage. "We are over. We've been over for two years. I don't want to see you; I don't want to hear from you. If you can't get the message, Catalina, you'll be hearing from my lawyer. And it won't be good."

Catalina isn't used to hearing the word 'no' from me. Her mouth falls open in shock. "Are you seeing someone?" she calls out to me. "I know you, Ethan. It won't last. I give it a month."

I don't reply. I need to find Maggie.

21

MAGGIE

E than's kissing his ex-wife, supermodel Catalina Hughes, and I feel like the biggest fool in the world.

Stupid, *stupid* Maggie. I should have known they were out of my league.

I pull my comforter around me. It's not a chilly night, but I can't seem to get warm. My body is wracked with shivers, and my hands are ice-cold.

There's a banging at the downstairs door. Either Lars or Ethan, I think bitterly, but I make no move to let them in. I have nothing to say to them.

"Maggie." Lars' voice carries clearly in the night air. "I can stand here and shout all night."

Damn him. He knows full well that I can't let that happen. New Summit is a gossipy little town, and by the morning, every single person will know that Lars Johansen was yelling outside Maggie Zhang's window at midnight. *Including my mother.*

My lips tightening, I stomp downstairs and open the

door. Both Lars and Ethan are standing there. "I don't want to talk to you," I snap. "Go away."

"We're either talking upstairs, or we're talking here," Ethan says firmly. "You decide."

I'm so angry my hands are shaking. "Fine." I turn around and head back upstairs. They follow me. When they get to my living room, Lars looks around, his attention caught by the photos on display. He picks up a photo of Lilly and I and examines it. "You have a twin sister? I didn't know that."

"Are you here to make small talk?"

Ethan runs his fingers through his hair. "You saw the kiss," he says quietly. "Please let me explain."

"I don't want to hear your excuses, Ethan," I reply, folding my arms over my chest. "We made no promises to each other. You don't have to stand here and lie to me." I blink my eyes furiously, willing the tears away. "Just leave."

"Please, Maggie." I've never seen a more serious look on Ethan's face. He looks almost anguished. "Just hear me out. Give me five minutes. At the end of it, I promise I'll leave."

Life Rule Number 4: Don't get involved with cheaters. I sigh heavily. "I know what I saw, Ethan." I cross over and sit down on the couch, and I don't look at the dark-haired man. I'm so angry right now, I could scream.

"Five minutes, Maggie. *Please?*"

"Fine," I reply grudgingly. I turn my head in Lars' direction. He's been watching the two of us silently. "Do you want a drink?"

"Sure." I grab the blond man a beer from my refrigerator and take a seat on the couch. Lars sits next to me, and Ethan wisely sits across the room on an armchair. "I was crazy about Catalina," he says. "I was the happiest person in the world when she agreed to marry me." His lips twist into a grimace. "Right from the start, our marriage was a disaster.

Catalina wanted to party every single night with her friends. She couldn't understand that I had to work. We fought constantly, and by the end, we were both bitterly unhappy."

"You looked cozy enough," I say before I can stop myself. "You didn't seem bitterly unhappy when she was pawing you."

He doesn't take the bait. "A year after the divorce was finalized, Lars and I sold the company we'd founded for a ton of money. Suddenly, Catalina was very interested in me again."

"She's a gold-digging bitch," Lars snaps.

Ethan ignores him as well. "I'd like to tell you that I turned her down, but that would be a lie. I've drunk-dialed Catalina for sex; she's done the same to me. But," he draws a deep breath. "The last time we slept together was six months ago."

"Why did you kiss her today?"

"I didn't. She took me by surprise."

I make a scoffing sound, and Ethan's dark eyes rest on me. "Maggie, you and I have slept together once. I don't have any reason to lie to you. Catalina wants to rekindle things, but I don't. I'm not interested in my ex-wife, Maggie. I'm interested in you."

I stare at him, uncertain about how to proceed. *Sleep with them,* my libido urges, but I ignore it. My hormones had been in charge Thursday night, but they're not running the show now.

Ethan is right. We slept together once—he really doesn't need to lie to me. I'm honestly surprised he's here, offering me an explanation. He doesn't owe me one. "I believe you," I say slowly. "But I don't think we should see each other again."

"Why not?" Lars' eyes bore into mine.

I play with a strand of my hair. "Look, you guys, Thursday night was great. But this can't go anywhere. I cannot tell my mother I'm in a ménage. She won't take the news well."

"So don't tell her," Lars replies.

I laugh harshly. "You don't know small towns, do you? If I start seeing you, someone will find out, and then, everyone will know. That's just the way it is here, and I won't hurt my family."

Lars' lips tighten. "Why have we never heard about your twin?" he demands.

I blink at the abrupt topic change. "My mother and Lilly got into an argument after my father died. Lilly didn't want to want to work at China Garden. They don't talk."

"So you're afraid," Ethan replies. "You don't want to rock the boat. You gave up your career for your family, and you're now ready to give up the rest of your life as well. When are you going to start living for yourself, Maggie?"

"Fuck you." My hands ball into fists. "You don't have it all figured out. You let Catalina kiss you. So don't offer me opinions about my life. Don't pretend to understand me or my family."

Ethan's jaw clenches. "I apologize," he says. "I shouldn't have said that. You're right. I don't understand your family dynamics; how can I?"

Lars' fingers trail up my leg, and I stiffen. "Your mother isn't here," he says softly. "Catalina isn't here. This is neither about the future nor past. We're alone, Maggie, There's just the three of us. So tell me, what do you want tonight?"

I should be sensible and send them away. I should hold on to my anger about Catalina. I should go to bed alone.

"You," I whisper. "Tonight, I want you."

LARS DOESN'T STOP STROKING my leg. The bottle clinks as he sets it down on the floor, and he leans in for a kiss.

His lips taste like beer. I whimper as his mouth crushes mine, and then I'm kissing him back as if my life depends on it. My hands run over his broad, muscled chest and my fingers play with the buttons on his shirt.

I can't resist them, I realize. It doesn't take much for lust to swallow me.

When we break away, my chest rises and falls like I've run a mile. I shift in my seat, pushing closer to him, ready to crawl in his lap for more.

Ethan rises to his feet and kneels in front of me. "I'm sorry about Catalina," he says. "Will you forgive me?"

I bite my lip. Lars' arm slides along my shoulders, a warm and comforting weight. "Maybe you should make it up to her," he suggests to Ethan.

I like that idea. A lot. "What about your guests?" I worry. "You can't miss your party."

Ethan shrugs. "The party's almost over. Katherine will take care of the stragglers." He cocks his head. "I'm exactly where I want to be, Maggie. Let me show you how sorry I am?"

"I don't know..." I don't want to appear too eager. "What did you have in mind?"

In another minute, my skirt is pushed up, my panties are pulled down, and I'm on my back on the couch, my legs draped over Ethan's shoulders as his mouth explores my mound.

Anytime Ethan wants to apologize this way, I'm on board.

Lars' hands cup my breasts and squeezes as he continues to kiss me. My blood pounds in my head under the onslaught. Being touched by two guys at the same time is so intense, so overwhelming, so *addictive*.

"You taste so good," Ethan tells me before putting his mouth on me again. He knows just how to work his lips and fingers, heating me up and driving me towards the edge with little flicks of his tongue against my clit.

"Fuck." My head falls back against the cushion. Lars catches my nipple in his teeth, and I arch my back, pushing my breast into his mouth. Pleasure threatens to blank my mind, and sensation overwhelms me.

I writhe and thrash on the couch, my body bucking against Ethan's tongue, and Lars catches my wrists, holding me down. "Don't fight it, Maggie," Lars whispers into my ear. "Let us pleasure you."

My eyes roll back in my head as Ethan drives his fingers into my tight pussy while keeping up the assault on my clitoris. It's too much. My insides twist and my muscles quiver and tremble, and my climax hurtles toward me, and I go over.

"Wow," I say weakly when I can breathe again. "That was amazing. I like the way you apologize."

Ethan sits next to me, and he licks his fingers. "Such a tasty treat," he says. My cheeks go pink at his words, but at the same time, heat ripples through me at the sight of him enjoying my taste.

Lars chuckles. "We're just getting started," he says. He gets to his feet and removes his clothes, unbuttoning his shirt, unbuckling his belt and unzipping his fly. I watch greedily as his naked body comes into view. "Open your mouth, Maggie."

His cock points at me, straight, long, stiff, and ready. I lick my lips and reach for his length. "Suck me," he orders, but he doesn't need to. I'm already running my tongue over his head, eager to taste him. Almost purring, I position myself on the edge of the couch and open my mouth. Placing my hands on his hips to steady myself, I eagerly take him all the way to the back of my mouth.

"Fuck," he groans, his eyes staring at me. "Oh fuck, Maggie. You are so beautiful." His fingers stroke my hair, but for the moment, he seems content to let me set the pace.

I lick from the base of his cock to his velvety smooth head, holding his gaze in mine. He throws his head back in a groan, and his eyes clench shut.

Ethan's hands cup my breasts, and he squeezes them as I bob my head on Lars' shaft. But after a few minutes, he gets up. "Stand up, Maggie," he orders. "Let's get you repositioned. I want your tight little pussy. I've thought of nothing else since Thursday night. All day, I've been hard thinking about you."

I stand up, trying to clear the fog from my brain. "There's condoms in the bathroom."

Ethan goes to get them. He returns in a minute with the box of condoms and a small bottle of lube. "How old is this thing?" he asks dubiously.

"I bought it at the drugstore yesterday," I admit, my cheeks flaming. "I also ordered a butt plug on the Internet."

"Exploring without us, Maggie?" Lars asks, his lips quirking up. "You're hurting my feelings, sweetheart."

"Take your clothes off," Ethan orders as he strips off his shirt. "And get your mouth back on Lars' cock."

Well, okay then, Mr. Bossy-Pants.

I wrap my lips around Lars' cock. "That's it," he breathes, his fingers twining in my hair. "Keep sucking."

His orders only make me hotter. My nipples bead, aching to be touched. Ethan reads my body perfectly, one hand pulling on the hardened nubs, the other still playing between my legs.

"So wet, Maggie," he says, his voice raspy with desire. "We're going to fuck you so thoroughly that you'll have trouble walking in the morning, sweetheart. We're going to take you in your pussy and in your ass, and you're going to beg and plead for more."

"Yes," I gasp. I hear the sound of the condom wrapper tear, then Ethan thrusts into me, his thick, hard cock filling my hungry pussy.

Arousal curls in my belly. My body blazes wherever the men touch me. I'm engulfed in raw heat as Ethan's length pounds my pussy, as Lars takes my mouth.

Ethan grabs a handful of my hair. My pussy gushes at the possessive gesture. "You think I want to kiss someone else, Maggie?" He laughs breathlessly. "You have no competition, sweetheart."

In this moment, I believe him. His fingers grip my hips, and his voice is rough and strained. My brain turns to mush, and my thoughts are shrouded in a haze of need. In this moment, there's just the three of us, lost in pleasure, clinging to each other as passion overtakes us. In this moment, I belong to them, just as surely as they belong to me.

Lars pulls free. "I want your ass, Maggie," he tells me.

"Yes," I pant, every fiber in my body craving to be filled completely by the two of them. I'm not afraid; I'm not nervous. *I'm ready.*

"In the bedroom," Ethan says.

We move to my bed, and Ethan lies down and pulls me on top of him. "Ride me."

I lower myself onto his length. It's so good. Ethan's shaft penetrates deep into my core, and it's intense. Overwhelming. Ethan's hands grip my breasts, squeezing them, pinching and tugging at my nipples as I lift myself up and down, grinding into his hard cock. My insides twist, and my muscles contract. Raw need claws through me.

Lars moves behind me. His fingertips stroke my back. A dollop of cool lube trickles between my butt cheeks. Ethan distracts me by tracing circles around my clitoris, and then I feel Lars' cock nudge at my tight hole.

My orgasm takes me by surprise. One moment, I'm nervous about being filled by them, and the next moment, I'm flailing, twisting, screaming as my climax rushes over me in an explosive wave.

Lars pushes in slowly, steady and unrelenting. I inhale sharply, and my fingers grip Ethan's shoulders as my muscles stretch to accommodate his thickness. "Almost there," Lars says, stroking my back gently. "Do you want me to stop?"

"No." The discomfort has subsided, and I relax once again. Lars slides in deeper, and then his entire length is in me.

Oh. My. God. They're both in me.

I'm a bad, *bad* girl. And I love it.

They start to move, slowly at first, and then picking up speed. "Touch yourself," Ethan orders. "I want to feel you come again, Maggie."

I reach down for my tight bundle of nerves, petting myself gently as the two men thrust

into me. They're sliding into me in unison, both pulling out of me, then plunging back in.

My body starts to shiver. Pleasure builds once again, a tight pressure that coils tighter, tighter, twisting my insides into a hard knot of desire. I can't hold on, but I want to. I want to feel them come first.

They're close. "You're so fucking tight," Lars pants, his fingers gripping my hips. "I'm going to come, Maggie."

Ethan's face is contorted with lust. His hands tighten around my waist, then he groans, long and low and deep, as he explodes. Lars is only an instant behind, and then I free-fall into release, almost sobbing with the intensity of my orgasm.

We stay huddled together in one sated, exhausted heap. *Catalina doesn't get to have this*, I think, as Ethan hugs me tight. But my satisfaction is short-lived.

I can't have them either.

22

LARS

"Let us take you out," I frown at Maggie, wishing that the woman Ethan and I are dating wasn't so stubborn. "Drinks, dinner, dancing."

She shakes her head. She's got her head on Ethan's lap and her feet on mine, and the three of us are watching Netflix in my living room. "I've told you already," she says, smiling to soften the sting of her words, "I can't. Nothing in public."

We've slept together a dozen times in the last two weeks, but she won't go out with us in public. Maggie doesn't want her mother and brother to find out about her ménage.

We're Maggie Zhang's dirty little secret, and I don't like it.

"I still don't see why you can't tell Dominic." I know I'm pouting, but I can't help it. I've never felt this way about anyone in my life. I thought the ménage would be weird, but that hasn't been an issue either. "Your brother likes us."

The secrecy, on the other hand? I chafe at it. I don't like that Maggie sneaks over to our place after dark. I hate that she never spends the entire night in our beds, lest someone sees her leave in the morning.

Maggie grins slyly. "That's because you let him drive your car."

"Your mom likes us too," Ethan interjects.

Maggie sits up. "What do you mean, my mom likes you?" There's a note of panic in her voice. "What did you tell her?"

I frown at Ethan. "Sweetie, calm down. China Garden is across the street. We get take-out there a lot when we're working late."

"And she likes you because you order food?" There's a worried look in her eyes.

"She likes us because we know Chinese food. We asked for beef with bok choi instead of broccoli, and she started talking to us. Now, whenever we go there, we get food that isn't on the menu."

A tiny smile appears on Maggie's lips. "Broccoli's not a Chinese vegetable," she concedes. "It's one of her pet peeves."

I stroke her back. "We don't like being a secret, Maggie," I tell her. "But neither Ethan nor I am going to tell your mother about our relationship. Not until you're ready."

She doesn't meet my eyes. "Our relationship?"

"What do you think this is?" Ethan asks her. "We've spent almost every night together for the past two weeks. I'm not sleeping with anyone else. Neither is Lars, and neither are you."

She exhales. "I don't put a name on it."

"Well, I do." I lace my fingers in hers. "I'm crazy about you, Maggie May. I don't want to see anyone else."

"That goes for me too," Ethan says.

She bites her lower lip. "Really?" she asks.

"What do you want from us, Maggie?" Maybe I'm fooling

myself here. After all, Maggie wrote dirty stories about us. Maybe she sees this thing between us as a fling. "Are you looking for something serious, or is this just about sex?"

"Not anymore." She looks troubled, but her grip on my hand tightens. "I really like both of you. I want to be in a relationship with you."

"Yet you're not smiling," Ethan points out.

She sighs deeply. "I'm afraid to tell my mother about our relationship," she admits. "She hasn't spoken to Lilly in three years. What if that happens to me?"

Ethan puts his arm around her shoulder. "We're here for you, Maggie," he says gently. "You can count on us."

23

MAGGIE

I've thrown all my life rules out of the window. I think I'm starting to fall in love with Lars and Ethan, and I don't know what to do about it. Will my mother cut me out of her life when she finds out about them, the way she did with my sister? I don't know.

I leave their place, deeply preoccupied. All day at the restaurant, I cook on auto-pilot. Lars and Ethan won't be patient with me forever. Sooner or later, they'll move on and start dating someone without as many issues as me. If I want to keep them, I'm going to have to tell my family the truth.

In the evening, instead of going home, I head across town to the basement apartment Dominic rents from Mrs. Manford. I knock on the door, and my brother opens it, looking surprised to see me. "Is mom okay?" he demands.

"Of course, Mr. Jumping-to-Conclusions. I wanted to talk to you."

He steps aside. I enter and take a seat on his futon. "Assuming the worst case scenario is an Asian thing," he says with a grin. "I can't help it."

"Oh, I don't know. Nina and Becky tell me their families

do it too." I take a deep breath. "I wanted to talk to you about something."

He frowns. "I'm going to tell mom about not going back to school," he says. "Soon. I promise. As soon as her birthday is over, I'll break the bad news to her."

"Don't want to rock the boat before the party?" I guess astutely. "That's not what I came over to tell you. I'm dating Lars and Ethan."

"Both of them? Like Ben and Landon and Mia?"

Oh right. Sophia, Landon's sister, is Dominic's friend. "Yeah."

"Huh. And you're serious about both men? You don't want to pick one of them?" Dominic's tone is maddeningly neutral, and I don't know what to make of his reaction.

I can't choose between them. Do I give up Lars, who always makes sure there's something to eat on the days I go over after working a long shift? Or Ethan, who reads my moods better than anyone and always knows what to say when I'm down?

Not that choosing one of them is really an option. Ethan and Lars are best friends. I can't destroy their friendship.

"Not really."

"Do they treat you well?" he asks.

"Yeah."

"Okay." He gives me a lopsided grin. "I like Lars and Ethan," he says. "If you're happy, then I'm happy for you. But Maggie," his voice turns serious, "You know mom's not going to take this well, right?"

I do. "I'm going to tell her." I chew on my bottom lip. "After the party."

I'm not afraid, I tell myself. I'm lying.

24

ETHAN

A few days after Maggie tells Dominic that she's dating both of us, we attend the next business association meeting. Maggie presents the findings, and the mayor looks quite enthusiastic by the amount of revenue similar events have brought into other small towns. "I think we should do it," he says, looking around the table. "What do you think?"

Dr. Bollington immediately protests, as do Mrs. Fischer and Mrs. Marshall, but the three of them are a minority. The matter is put to the vote and the night market wins easily. "Excellent," the mayor says. He looks at Lars and Maggie. "I'd like the two of you to run the event," he says. "Maggie, you know everyone in New Summit, and Lars can give you a hand. What do you think?"

Lars' lips twitch. "I think you just volunteered us, Mr. Wagner."

He grins, unrepentant. "If I sat around waiting for volunteers, we'd never get anything done. So, what do you think? Will you do it?"

Maggie's nodding her head when my phone buzzes. I glance at the display. Natalie.

Our assistant knows our schedule; she knows we're in a meeting. She wouldn't disturb us if it weren't an emergency. I murmur an apology to the others and step outside to call her back. "What's the matter?" I ask when she picks up the phone.

"You might have a problem," she says. "After Catalina crashed our last party, I hired detectives to keep an eye on her."

"You did what? Natalie, as irritating as my ex-wife is, I don't think we should be invading her privacy."

"Can you yell at me later? The detective just called me. Catalina took the exit to New Summit ten minutes ago." She takes a deep breath. "If she's found out about Maggie…"

My blood turns to ice. Maggie has been hiding our affair from her mother. Catalina can be shrewd when she needs to be, and I told her that I was seeing someone else. She even saw both Lars and I run after Maggie that night. If she put her mind to it, it wouldn't have taken her too long to find out who I'm dating.

The meeting must have broken up because a handful of people exit the coffee shop, Maggie and Lars among them. "What's wrong?" Maggie asks the moment she sees my face.

"I think we have a problem."

25

MAGGIE

I don't have the luxury of waiting for the perfect moment. I need to tell my mother about Lars and Ethan now, before his evil witch of an ex-wife does something stupid.

I practically run down the block from Cassie's coffee shop to China Garden, Ethan and Lars at my heels. But it's too late. When I get to the restaurant, Catalina is already there. She's wearing a short, tight red dress, her hair is wildly disheveled, and she looks like she's been drinking. "There you are," she says dramatically when I walk in. It's three in the afternoon. There's a young Indian couple eating a late lunch, but the restaurant is empty except for them. The supermodel turns to my mother and her voice rises. "Are you aware," she says, pointing an accusing finger at me. "That your daughter has been lying to you for more than a month?"

Angela Zhang looks confused. "Who are you?" she asks, her voice sounding mystified. "What are you talking about?"

Ethan enters the restaurant, pinning his ex-wife with his

eyes. "Catalina, I'm warning you," he says coldly. "If you don't leave here right now, *there will be consequences.*"

She lifts her chin up. "What do you see in her?" she sneers. "She's a fucking cook in a shitty Chinese restaurant."

"Shut the fuck up, Catalina," Lars snarls, his face contorted with rage. "Unlike Maggie, you've never done one decent, unselfish thing in your life. Maggie's worth a hundred of you."

My mother is looking from Lars to Ethan to Catalina to me, awareness and a dreadful suspicion slowly dawning on her face. "Maggie," she addresses me, her voice whisper-quiet, "What's going on here?"

Now, Maggie. If there was ever a time for the truth, it's now.

My heartbeat accelerates. I love my mother. Yes, she can be entirely too involved in the life of her children, but I've always been loved, always been cherished by my parents. Lars might call me unselfish, but I know different. Because the words I'm about to say will break my mother's heart.

"Ma," I start, but Catalina, that fucking bitch, interrupts me before I can say anything else. "Isn't it obvious?" she says bitterly. "Your daughter, *your precious, decent, unselfish daughter,* is sleeping with both Lars and Ethan. At the same time."

My mother's face goes slack with shock. "Maggie," she asks, a distinct tremble in her voice, "Is this true?"

I feel the solid presence of Lars and Ethan behind me. Warm and reassuring. *We're here for you, Maggie,* Ethan said last week. *You can count on us.*

Catalina's watching, an unpleasant smile playing on her lips. I want to throatpunch her, but what's the point? The damage has been done. My mother's looking at me as if I've suddenly grown a second head. I take a deep breath. "Yes," I reply, my voice clear. "I was afraid to tell you," I admit. "But it's true. I'm dating both Lars and Ethan."

My mother sinks into a chair. "I thought I raised you to be a decent woman." Her face is pale and her voice trembles with emotion. "Where did I go wrong?"

I swallow the lump in my throat. "I love them, Ma," I say pleadingly. "I know it's not conventional, but I really care about them. I hope you can be happy for me."

I've said the wrong thing. "Be happy for you?" Her jaw tightens. "You come to me and tell me you are sleeping with two men, and you want me to be happy?"

Out of the corner of my eye, I see Dominic standing by the kitchen door, watching the scene unfold in front of him. "Ma," he intercedes on my behalf, "So what if Maggie's seeing Ethan and Lars? They're nice guys. Who's she hurting anyway?"

"Me." Angela Zhang's voice is cold. "She's hurting me." She looks at me, her lips pursed in a thin, disapproving line. "End this nonsense, Maggie."

I can feel Lars and Ethan stiffen behind me. "I won't." I try one last appeal. "Ma, please. They're good men. Won't you give them a chance?"

She shakes her head. "Get out of my restaurant, Maggie, and don't come back." She pivots on her heels and walks into the kitchen, pushing my brother out of the way as she does.

Dominic stares at me helplessly. Neither of us knows what to do.

It hurts to breathe. My eyes fill with tears, and I blink them away, not wanting Ethan's ex-wife to see me cry. I'm so furious that I want to scratch her eyes out. "You thought I would break up with them?" I snarl at her. "You thought I'd dump them because my mother asked me to?"

Lars folds me into his arms. Hidden in his embrace, I let the tears fall. Ethan addresses his ex-wife, his voice icy. "I warned you to stay away from us, Catalina. You went too far. I'm going to destroy you."

I broke all my rules for love. I'm not sure I did the right thing.

26

LARS

Maggie can't stop shivering. We bundle her into the shower and climb in with her, so she isn't alone. After the hot water has rained down on her for almost thirty minutes, she finally takes a deep breath and smiles at us tremulously. "Sorry about that," she says. "Family drama."

"Are you okay, sweetie?" I ask.

"I could kill Catalina," Ethan grinds out at the same time.

"I'm fine," she says to me. "Yup, she's a troublemaking bitch," she says to Ethan.

Ethan pours a dollop of shower gel on a washcloth and lathers Maggie's body. "I'm sorry," he says. "She left me alone for three weeks. I thought she'd finally got the message. I guess I thought wrong."

"Mmm." There's an expression of pleasure on her face as Ethan caresses her breasts.

"Are you sure you're okay?" I insist. Maggie loves her family. She talks to her sister every day. She works with her mother and her brother. After today's events, things will change.

"I've been dreading telling my mother for three weeks," she replies. "At least it's over. In a weird way, I'm almost relieved." Biting her lower lip, she looks at me. "I don't want to think about it tonight. Want to go out for dinner?"

"Outside?" Ethan's expression softens. "Where people can see us?"

"No need to hide anymore," she quips. "You kept threatening to buy me dinner. How about now?"

"Okay." I kiss the back of her neck, the spot that makes her flush with pleasure. "But we can't go yet." I guide her hand to my erection. "We have to take care of this first."

"Of course." Her hand closes over my shaft, and she strokes up and down my length. "We can't have you wandering around town in such a state. New Summit would be scandalized."

27

MAGGIE

Their hands tip me back on the bed. My hair spreads all over the pillowcase, wild and tangled, and Ethan's lips lift in a small smile. "Your hair was like this the day you almost towed Lars' car," he says. "I'd seen you before that, of course, but that was the day I really saw you."

His lips trail kisses over my shoulder. "You were standing with your hands folded over your chest," he says, laughter in his tone, "Your tits pushed up, and I could take my eyes off your nipples."

"My nipples?"

Lars chuckles. "You weren't wearing a bra," he says. "Your nipples were pebbled. Don't wear a white shirt, sweetheart."

I punch him on the bicep, my cheeks flaming. "You were ogling me," I accuse.

"Guilty," Ethan replies with a wide smile. "You were so fucking hot, and you had no clue. I couldn't stop thinking of you."

I snort to hide my pleasure. "Oh come on. If you were interested in me, you'd have made a move."

"Nope," Lars replies. "Neither of us would have made a move. I knew Ethan was interested in you, and he knew I was. We weren't going to get in each other's way."

"And then we found your dirty stories," Ethan whispers into my ear. "And we realized that we didn't need to compete."

Lars kisses me, warm and soft. My breath catches in a hitch. "So beautiful," he murmurs. His hands cup my breasts, and he lowers his mouth over my nipples. "You like that, sweetheart?"

My brain is starting to short-circuit with pleasure. I run my hands over them, savoring their broad chests, their tight muscles, the taut firmness of their bodies, and the warmth of their skin.

They're mine.

"Take me," I whisper.

"So soon, Maggie?" Ethan's eyes dance with dark amusement. "You're in such a hurry, baby. Where's the fun in that?"

Right. I'm going to have to take matters into my own hands. I bend down and take Lars' thick cock in my mouth, arching my hips into Ethan's face.

He chuckles and takes the hint. "I love the way you taste, Maggie," he says. He spreads my legs wide and attacks my pussy with raw, unbridled passion. His tongue licks a long, slow trail up my slit, then he concentrates his attention on my clitoris, sliding two fingers inside my pussy at the same time.

Whimpering with need, I close my fingers around the base of Lars' shaft, stroking him while I suck him. Ethan's fingers twist and turn inside me, pressing down on my g-spot, driving me wild with desire.

I'm crazy about them. Whatever the consequences, I can't give them up. My need for them is deep and reckless and all-consuming.

I love them.

My muscles clench, tighten. A familiar spiral of longing overtakes me. My release sweeps over me in a wave of pleasure, and I surrender to it.

Afterward, I bury my face in Lars' shoulder while Ethan presses against my back. "So," Ethan says slowly. "At the restaurant earlier, you told your mother you were in love with us."

Oh God. I was hoping they hadn't heard that. "Mmm," I mutter, my cheeks on fire. "Does that freak you out?"

Lars' hand trails a slow, languid path down my torso. "Do we look freaked out?" he asks. His fingers tease my nipples lazily. "I was really glad to hear you say it," he admits softly. "I'm in love with you, Maggie. It's been hard keeping our relationship a secret. I'm crazy about you, and I want to shout it from the rooftops."

"Me too." Ethan kisses my shoulder. "After Catalina, I didn't think I'd ever fall in love again." His grip tightens around my waist. "Then you exploded into our lives like a force of nature."

My heart overflows with happiness, but my joy is bittersweet. I love Ethan and Lars. If I had to go back in time, I'd make the same decisions all over again.

Unfortunately, the best relationship of my life has come at a cost. My mother wants nothing to do with me.

28

MAGGIE

The next few days are surreal. I show up to the restaurant as usual, unsure if I've been fired, but my mother doesn't demand I leave. Though we work side-by-side, my mother doesn't say a word to me, giving me the silent treatment. "The only child she's still talking to is you," I tell Dominic sadly after one never-ending eight-hour shift, during which my mother didn't say a single word to me.

"Not for long." He grimaces at me. "She said something the other day about me going back to school in the fall. I've got to tell her soon."

I shake my head. "Are we bad people? You, me, Lilly?"

Dominic puts his arm around me. "She wants the best for us, that's all. She'll come around."

"Is Patrick still throwing her the birthday party?"

"Yes." He gives me a stern look. "And you're still invited, so don't think about missing it."

"I don't know if you noticed, Dominic, but she hasn't said a word to me all week. I don't want to ruin the party."

"You have to be there, Maggie. Family is important."

I sigh. Family *is* important, but nothing about this situation is easy. "I know."

IT'S the day of the party. I'm going through the contents of my closet, trying to find something to wear. Lars and Ethan are sitting on my bed, watching me with a bemused expression on their faces, when my phone rings. It's Patrick.

"Let me guess," I say lightly, though my heart is heavy in my chest. "You think it's best that I stay away."

"On the contrary, I was calling to invite Lars and Ethan."

"What?" Ethan and Lars look up at my squeak. "You don't think that's just going to add fuel to the fire?"

"Are you going to stop dating them, Maggie?" Patrick asks. "No, you aren't. Well, bring them. Your mother will deal with it."

"You don't know my mother very well if you think she's going to deal with it," I reply. "Has she ever mentioned Lilly to you?"

"Many times," he replies unexpectedly. "And I wanted it to be a surprise, but Lilly and her boyfriend Seth are coming to the party. They flew down yesterday and spent the night in Manhattan. They're probably on the road now, on their way to New Summit."

I suck in a breath of air. "You invited Lilly to the party? Patrick, you like to live dangerously, don't you?"

He huffs in laughter. "Maggie, I'm not going to be arrogant enough to suggest I know your mother better than you do," he says gently. "But I do know that I see a different side of her. Angela and I, we're both parents who've raised children we're very proud of. That gives us something in common."

"Hang on a second, let me find out if they want to come." I cover the phone with my hand and look at Lars and Ethan. "Patrick just invited you to the party tonight."

"We'd love to go," Ethan replies at once. "What can we bring?"

THE PARTY IS ALREADY UNDERWAY when we arrive fifteen minutes late. My mother, Dominic, Cassie, and Lucas are sitting at a picnic table in the backyard, amiably chatting with each other. James and Patrick are hovering over the grill.

"Happy birthday, mom." I give her the present I bought her, a blue dress that she'd seen in Mia's shop window that she'd loved.

"Thank you," she says stiffly.

Two words. That's progress, right.

Cassie jumps in to rescue us before things can get awkward. "Maggie, I love your shirt," she says. "Ethan, Lars, welcome. There's beer and white wine in the coolers, and red wine inside the house."

"Happy Birthday, Angela." Lars smiles warmly at my mother. "Nice party."

"I didn't know Patrick was planning anything," she replies. Her expression softens when she looks at James' father. "I don't usually celebrate my birthday."

"We brought champagne." Ethan holds out three bottles in my mother's direction.

My mother doesn't answer him. She's looking straight ahead. I turn my head to see what she's starting at, and I see my twin Lilly standing at the garden gate, a tall man with long black hair at her side. "Happy birthday, mom."

Dominic notices Lilly too, and the two of us brace for a

scene. Poor Patrick, I think. He was just trying to do a nice thing.

Patrick comes over to my mom. He puts his arm around her waist. "I know you miss her," he says, his voice quiet. "Stop being stubborn, Angela. Life's too short. Go make nice."

To my total, utter shock, my mom doesn't look angry at his words, and she doesn't leave the party. Her eyes fill with tears, and she gets to her feet, and she envelops my sister in a hug. "Lilly Rose," she says, her voice thick with emotion. "You came to my birthday party."

My mouth falls open. Dominic looks like someone hit him with a baseball bat. Patrick sits down next to us, looking smug. "How did you know she'd be okay?" Dominic asks. "I thought mom would freak out."

"The two of you didn't tell me about Lilly," he replies. "Angela did. Your mother wanted to end the estrangement. She was just too afraid to take the first step. So I did."

I hug Patrick tightly. "Thank you."

He smiles at me, warm and serene. Patrick's survived a stroke that almost killed him. He's among the nicest people I know. I'm really happy that my mother's seeing him.

This reconciliation between my mother and sister feels like a miracle. Is it too much to expect one of my own?

AN HOUR LATER, the party is in full swing. I'm chatting with Lilly and her partner Seth when I notice Dominic pull my mother aside to a corner of the garden. The two of them spend fifteen minutes in conversation, and when they're done, Dominic has an expression of relief on his face. "He told her he doesn't want to go back to law school," I whisper to Lars and Ethan. "She seems to have taken the news well."

"Go talk to her," Lars nudges me as Dominic wanders back to the main table. "You know you want to."

"Yeah." I take a deep breath. I'm not Lilly. I don't want to spend the next three years ignoring my mother's existence. As difficult as this conversation is going to be, I need to have it.

Getting to my feet, I fill my glass with champagne for courage and walk over. My mother's staring into the distance. "Hey," I say as I near her. "So Lilly's here."

Angela Zhang nods. "Dominic already told you he wanted to run the restaurant."

"Yeah."

Her lips twist. "We came to America with almost no money, and we worked fifteen hours a day. We wanted a better life for our children." She sighs deeply. "Your father wanted Dominic to be a doctor or a lawyer. Instead, he's happy running a restaurant. Where did we go wrong?"

"He doesn't want to be a lawyer, Ma. I know you want him to be happy."

She sighs again. "Lilly's boyfriend seems nice."

"Yes," I say cautiously. "I think so." I take a deep drink from the glass in my hand. "Ma, I'm sorry. I should have told you about Lars and Ethan. You shouldn't have heard it from that woman."

She nods. "Your sister isn't drinking," she says, changing the topic. "She isn't saying anything yet, but I think she's pregnant."

"What?" I turn around and look at Lilly. Sure enough, although there's a glass of champagne next to her, she's not drinking from it. Seth is. "Wow, good eye."

"A mother sees these things." There's a long pause as she plays with the fringe on her shawl. "You're happy with them," she says.

"Yeah, I really am."

"I'm old-fashioned. Set in my ways. I don't understand why one man isn't good enough for you. Why do you need two?"

Ethan laughs at something Dominic says to him. Lars is talking to Cassie, animated and intense. My mother's asking me a question for which I don't have the answer. I only know what's in my heart. "I can't choose between them."

She bends down and pulls a dandelion from the grass. "I don't want to see any of those PDAs."

I laugh out loud. "You mean public displays of affection?" I shake my head fondly. "When did you discover that term?"

She rolls her eyes. "All children think their parents are oblivious." She waits for me to reply, her gaze expectant. *She's negotiating with me.* I realize there might be a way out of this impasse.

"No PDAs," I agree.

"I will pretend that they are your roommates," she adds.

"I want them to come to our family lunches," I counter.

She smiles unexpectedly. "They like food, those two. Not picky eaters. They can come to lunch."

My mother's never going to jump with joy at the thought of my relationship. But this is better than I'd hoped for. This is the best case scenario.

"See you on Monday."

BY UNSPOKEN AGREEMENT, we end up in Ethan's bedroom after the party. "Spend the night, Maggie?"

"I have to work tomorrow," I start, then I reconsider my words. Everything's out in the open. Lars and Ethan aren't a secret anymore. I smile widely, happier than I've ever been. "I'd love to."

EPILOGUE

Six months later...

Christmas is a time for family. Last year, Dominic, my mother, and I had opened presents around a hastily-decorated fake tree, and we didn't mention our missing sister.

This year, things are very different.

My mother was right. Lilly had been pregnant when she came to visit for Angela Zhang's birthday. She gave birth two months ago to a baby girl, Emily Rose. "Sticking to the flower theme?" I'd asked dryly, looking at the tiny bundle of joy my sister cradled in her arms.

She'd grinned and given me the middle finger. "At least I wasn't named after a Rod Stewart song," she'd retorted.

After Catalina outed our relationship at China Garden, Ethan was furious. He placed several phone calls the next day to his business contacts, his jaw tightly set. By the time he was done, Catalina had lost all her upcoming movie roles. The cosmetics company that she modeled for decided not to renew her contract, as did her modeling agency. In three months, she was completely out of work.

"Aren't you being a little vicious?" I'd asked Ethan, though to be honest, I wasn't really crying tears of sadness over Catalina's fate. Evil bitch.

The last I heard, she's moved to Australia for a fresh start. Thank heavens.

It's Christmas Eve. Cassie, James, and Lucas bravely volunteered to host us. The twelve foot tall Frasier Fir tree is decorated with red and white ornaments. Christmas carols play in a non-stop loop on the radio, and the house smells of cookies.

Best of all, our family has grown. This year, it's not just Dominic, my mom, and me. There's Patrick, James, Lucas, and Cassie. There's Dominic's new girlfriend, Jenny. Lilly's flown down with her fiancé, Seth, and two-month-old Emily Rose.

And of course, there's Ethan and Lars. My lovers and my best friends. I really couldn't be happier.

I DON'T WORK at China Garden anymore. Buoyed by the success of my first catering gig, I started a small catering company. "Oh thank heavens," Natalie had said when she found out. "New Summit needed a competent caterer. Consider yourself booked for ReadStream's first book launch."

"Natalie, I can't do that. I'm dating Ethan and Lars," I'd tried protesting.

The hyper-competent assistant had shrugged away my concerns. "Maggie," she'd said patiently. "I wouldn't hire you if you didn't do a good job. You're not getting this gig because you're sleeping with the bosses. Your food is delicious."

Business is good, much better than I expected. It turns out that Natalie was right—our town really did need a caterer. I've been hired for weddings, for birthday parties, and corporate events.

"Hey." Lilly wanders over and sits next to me. "Penny for your thoughts."

"I'm daydreaming," I confess. I look at my twin, an idea striking me. "Are you going to be able to keep working with Emily Rose?"

She sighs. "Not really. You know how crazy restaurant hours are. I can't juggle the baby and my job, and Seth doesn't make enough money for us to be able to live in the Bay area."

"Any thoughts on what you're going to do?"

She shakes her head. "We haven't had a spare moment in the last couple of months," she confesses. "We figured we'd make plans once we got back."

"Would you consider working for me?" I ask her. "I'm busier than I expected to be. Sophia's been helping me out, but she's starting culinary school next year. If you move back home, there'll be no shortage of help with the baby."

"Really?"

I nod. "If you want, there's a job for you here. But I totally understand if you want to stay at Stone Soup. I'm not a two-star Michelin restaurant."

Her lips twist into a wry smile. "I can't have both, Maggie," she says. "You know how many female Michelin-starred chefs have young children? Almost none. The ones that do are running family restaurants, so they have more job security. It's brutal and cutthroat, and if I want to stay in the game, I won't be able to watch Emily grow up."

"You're not sad?"

"A little," she admits wistfully. "I can't have everything, and I'd like to."

I put my arm around her shoulder. "Look at that cutie," I tell her. Ethan is holding Emily in his arms, and she's laughing and clutching his hair in her pudgy little grasp. "She's totally worth it."

Lilly smiles. "Totally," she echoes. "So, tell me about your hotties. Things still good?"

"Things are great," I reply at once. "Really, really great."

My sister grins slyly. "You never told me you wrote dirty stories about them." She shakes her head. "Maggie, Maggie, Maggie. How very naughty of you."

A blush creeps up my cheeks. I'm never going to live *Dirty Words* down. "Cassie told you?"

"Yup. Pity you took them down before I could read them. Then again, I know you have the hots for them, but I really don't want to picture Ethan and Lars naked."

"Please don't," I retort, but I'm biting back my smile. Lars and Ethan don't know it yet, but I've written another dirty story about them. Now, I have to make sure they find out about it.

"HELLO, MA."

It's after lunch and the party's winding down. I make my way to the corner of the room, where my mother's sitting in a rocking chair, knitting a sweater for Emily.

My mother smiles up at me and indicates the chair by her side, and I sit down. "So you offered Lilly a job, did you?" she asks. "That was kind of you."

"Not really. Lilly's a great chef. I'll be lucky to have her."

She pats my hand. "It's not good for your sister to be so

far away from her family," she says. "I'll be glad when she moves back home."

"*If*, mother. There's no guarantee she's going to take the offer. You're not going to meddle, are you?"

"I never meddle," she replies loftily, her needles clicking away busily.

I snort at the enormity of that lie, but it's Christmas, so I let it go. We sit in silence for a little while. "They'd make good fathers," she says, looking at Lars and Ethan.

I roll my eyes. "Your granddaughter is only two months old," I tell her severely. "I thought I'd have another year before you started dropping hints. Besides, according to you, Ethan and Lars are my roommates."

She gives me an exasperated look, and I return her gaze blandly. Her lips twitch. "Both my daughters are very headstrong women," she says.

"I wonder where we got that from."

She chuckles. "Your father, of course," she says. "He was a very stubborn man."

Dad was a pushover. For Patrick's sake, I hope he's made of sterner stuff.

WE GET BACK HOME at four in the afternoon. "I'm going to be in the garage," Lars announces.

"Of course," Ethan says dryly. "I'm sure there's something to polish. Maybe a speck of dust landed on one of the cars?"

I have to laugh at Lars' disgruntled expression. The truth is, I want both of them out of the living room so I can set my plan in motion. I have to load up my newest story on Dirty Words, and then leave my laptop in plain sight, so that they accidentally stumble upon my smutty fantasy.

"Why don't you go help Lars?" I suggest. "I'm going to take a shower, and then maybe I can give you your Christmas present?"

Ethan's eyebrows rise. "What Christmas present?" he asks suspiciously. "You wouldn't let us buy you anything. Did you break the rules, Maggie?"

I can't stop the smile from breaking out across my face. "Wait and see."

I NAVIGATE to the Dirty Words website and pull up the story I've written. I didn't use their names this time—Ethan has been renamed Evan, and Lars is now Liam—since I don't want to risk Natalie and Katherine finding the story. The first time was embarrassing enough.

I'm hoping that Lars and Ethan glance at my laptop screen and see the big Dirty Words logo. I position the computer, so the screen is visible from almost the entire living room.

Then, my heart beating in my chest, I go take a shower.

I'M DRYING my hair when I hear Ethan's voice call out my name. They've found my dirty story. "Maggie," he says. "Come here a minute, will you?"

"Just a second."

Black lace panties? Check.

White t-shirt, transparent enough that the outlines of my nipples are clearly visible? Check.

I head to the living room. "What's the matter?" I ask innocently. Yup, the two of them are looking at my laptop screen.

"I didn't realize you were reviving your writing career,

Maggie." Ethan sounds amused. "Already bored of your catering business?"

"We didn't read your story, Maggie," Lars says, his lips quirking into a grin. "We didn't want to invade your privacy. No, we had a better idea."

He points to the leather armchair. "Take your panties off, Maggie," he orders. "And sit on that chair."

Pinpricks of anticipation burst across my skin. I do as they ask, sliding my lace briefs down my hips. Ethan holds out his hand for them.

Crap. I'm wet already, and now, Ethan and Lars are going to find out.

Sure enough, Ethan examines the lace scrap in his hand. "Wet already, Maggie," he says, shaking his head in mock disapproval. "What a naughty girl you are." He steps back, his eyes running over my body. "Spread your legs wide, sweetheart. Show us how turned on you are."

A blush creeps up my neck as I part my legs shoulder-width apart. "Wider," Lars chides. "Hook your legs on the armrests, Maggie. I want to see that pretty little pussy of yours."

Ethan sets my laptop on the coffee table in front of me, close enough that the screen is clearly visible. "Read us your story, Maggie."

"Aloud?" There's a definite tremble in my voice.

"Yup." Ethan chuckles at my mortified expression. "What's the matter, sweetheart? You wrote it, after all."

I didn't think they'd make me read it out loud. I'm going to die of embarrassment.

"Stop delaying, Maggie."

I swallow the lump in my throat and start to read.

"Maggie was there for one thing, and one thing only. Sex. The

instant she walked through the door, Liam pounced on her. He pulled her wrists behind her back, and he cuffed them together."

"I'm Liam, am I?" Lars stalks toward me, a red scarf in his hands. "No cuffs, Maggie, so I'm going to have to improvise. Put your hands above your head."

He ties my wrists together, quickly and efficiently. I test the bonds when he's done, but there's no slack in them. "Umm, you're really good at this. Anything you want to tell me?"

"Keep reading, Maggie."

I read the next words.

"Evan gave her a searching glance. 'What do you want?' He asked her. She didn't answer him at first. She was ashamed of her needs."

"Never be ashamed of your needs, Maggie," Ethan says silkily. He drizzles some lube over my glass butt plug—the same one they used on me the first night—and he pushes it into my ass.

I whimper as the heavy wide plug fills me, and I read the next line.

"'Say it,' Evan told Maggie. 'Say you want me to make you come.'"

"This story moves rather quickly," Lars observes. "No chase, no foreplay. Jumping straight to the action."

"Everybody's a critic," I reply pertly.

They chuckle as I continue.

"'Your pussy's throbbing and soaked,' Liam said to Maggie. 'Do you want to come, baby?'"

Ethan unzips his pants and pulls his thick, fat, heavy cock out. I lick my lips automatically, unable to resist. "Let me show you how much I want to come," I purr at him.

"I should make you read the rest of the story," he says.

"We have all evening." I pinch my nipples through my shirt and Ethan and Lars inhale sharply.

"Bad girl," Lars says sternly. He gets naked too. His cock bobs at the entrance of my pussy, and I wriggle my hips, trying to get him to thrust into me. "All in due time, baby," he says, rubbing his head over my clitoris. "What's the hurry?"

Ethan squeezes my breasts and pinches my nipples. He bends down and sucks the hardened nubs through my t-shirt, and I gasp, unable to hold back my sound of pleasure.

"Stop teasing me," I groan, reaching for Ethan's cock. I close my fingers over his shaft, and I pump his length. I take him in my mouth, luxuriating in the taste of him, clean and male.

Lars grabs my hips and flips me so I'm on my knees. He fills my pussy in a forceful, powerful thrust, not stopping until his entire cock is buried deep inside me. The sensation of being so filled practically robs me of control, and before I know it, I'm slamming back against Lars to feel him bottoming out inside me.

The deep, blissful ache is like nothing else. As Lars pounds into me, Ethan leans back and grabs my head with both hands, thrusting deeper into my mouth.

The two gorgeous men are having their way with me, and I'm overwhelmed.

"Do you know what happens to bad girls who write dirty

stories," Lars grunts as he thrusts. "They get spanked." His palm connects with my ass in a firm slap.

"Yes," I hiss, throwing my head back with abandon. "Do that again."

He switches to the other side to give me a few firm strikes there.

My climax builds as they continue, my body slamming back and forth between them. Then Ethan grips my hair tightly, and he comes down my throat. Lars' grip on my hips tightens as he too explodes, and that's all it takes. I come in a bone-shattering orgasm.

We continue role-playing bits and pieces of my dirty story all evening. I drift off to sleep after my fifth toe-curling orgasm. When I wake up, Lars and Ethan are watching me. "What's the matter?" I ask them.

"You know how your mom keeps telling herself we're your roommates?" Lars asks.

I nod.

Ethan holds out a key. "Want to make it official?"

I don't have to think about my answer, not even for a second. "Yes," I reply, grinning widely, "I'd love to."

They kiss me tenderly, and I hug them tight.

I used to have a lot of rules governing my life. Now, I have only one. *Always take a chance on love.*

∾

Thank you for reading Maggie, Lars & Ethan's story! I hope you love them as much as I do.

∾

THE COCKY SERIES

Love small town menage romances? Try the COCKY SERIES, set in the quirky tourist town of Goat, Oregon. Turn the page for a free preview of Her Cocky Doctors!

THE DIRTY SERIES

Have you read all four Dirty books? Don't miss out. Each book has a heartwarming and steamy romance, snark and humor, and smoking' hot men determined to get their woman.

Dirty Therapy - Mia, Benjamin & Landon
Dirty Talk - Cassie, James & Lucas
Dirty Games - Nina, Scott & Zane
Dirty Words - Maggie, Lars & Ethan

Or, buy the collection for a discount...
Dirty - the Complete Collection

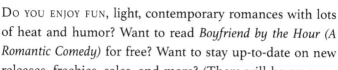

DO YOU ENJOY FUN, light, contemporary romances with lots of heat and humor? Want to read *Boyfriend by the Hour (A Romantic Comedy)* for free? Want to stay up-to-date on new releases, freebies, sales, and more? (There will be an occasional cat picture.) **Sign up to my newsletter!** You'll get the book right away, and unless I have a very important announcement—like a new release—I only email once a week.

A PREVIEW OF HER COCKY DOCTORS

PROLOGUE

Declan:

She's naked under the thin hospital gown, lying on her back, her feet dangling next to the stirrups at the end of the examination table.

Christmas came early this year.

She's beautiful, and she's ours. I want her soft pouty pink lips wrapped around my cock. I want to hear her moan my name, her large brown eyes hazy with need. I want to feel her muscles tremble as we make her come, over and over again.

I exchange a glance with Blake as the two of us move inside the room. When she hears us, her breathing quickens, but she stays where she is.

"Ms. Davey," I greet her, my gaze drawn to her round breasts. I can see the outline of her nipples under the thin robe, firm and erect, and my cock hardens in response. "What brings you in today?"

Her cheeks are pink and flushed. "I'd like the special service, Doctor," she whispers. "Will you make me feel good?"

Make me feel good. That's the code phrase. Lana Davey isn't here for a routine examination. She's here for the extra service this clinic offers. She's here for a 'happy ending'.

I'm delighted to oblige.

Blake moves to the foot of the bed. Before she has time to answer, he nudges her knees apart and positions her legs into the supports, spreading her wide open. While he does that, I reach behind her back and undo the tie that keeps the gown closed. "You won't need this today."

"Yes, Doctor." Her voice is barely audible in the quiet room as I pull away the gown, and she's exposed to my gaze.

She's absolutely gorgeous, and I can't resist her. Cupping her plump breasts in my hand, I squeeze them, and she moans in response. "Yes," she whimpers, throwing back her head, her hips bucking in need. "Oh God, that's so good."

"You know what I'm going to do, Ms. Davey?" Blake's voice is rough with desire. "I'm going to push my cock into your wet pussy. You're ready for me, aren't you?" His fingers tease her slit, hovering just out of reach of her clitoris, and she bites back another moan.

"Yes Doctor," she says again.

I squeeze her perfectly round breasts, rubbing her pert pink nipples between my thumb and forefinger. She's so beautiful, so responsive. Running my hands over her ankles, I make my way to the space between her legs. "Are you wet, Ms. Davey?" I scold her. "Already? You're such a bad girl."

Blake grasps her ankles and buckles them into the stirrups. Her breathing quickens as he places her, swiftly and surely, under his control. "Somebody's excited," he says, amused. He bends his mouth to Lana's pussy, and she whimpers as he sucks her clitoris between his teeth, almost jumping off the table in response.

"Tie her down, Declan," Blake says to me. "I don't want her squirming away from me."

A shiver runs through her body, as I hold up the leather straps in my hands so she can see them. Goosebumps rise on her skin, but her eyes shine with excitement, and she nods eagerly.

A smile curls on my lips.

Ms. Davey, we're about to give you an afternoon you're never going to forget.

≈

CHAPTER ONE

Lana:

I've never felt the urge to throttle my boss. Until now.

"You *promised* I could go on vacation." I stare at John Beene in exasperation.

For months, the managing editor of The Torch, Portland's finest investigative weekly news magazine, has had me chasing one depressing story after another. I've done exposés of isolated religious sects in which the 'leader' marries every fifteen-year-old girl in the community. I've written articles about corruption in local governments. About water poisoning. About factories in the remote Northwest breaking environmental regulations without consequences.

I'm exhausted. "I've been living out of a suitcase for the last three months," I continue, my voice rising in frustration.

"You promised me that I could take a week off, and you promised," I give my unrepentant boss a glare that bounces off him without impact, "that you'd give me a stint in the Lifestyle department. Three months, I believe you said."

"That was before the Pulitzer nomination," John says blandly. "Come on, Lana. You're an amazing investigative journalist. I have a story for you to investigate. I don't see what the problem is."

Let's see. When I got back to my apartment after chasing the latest story, my lone houseplant, a cactus, had died. Cacti survive in deserts. They're supposedly indestructible, but even a cactus couldn't survive my neglect. "John," I try to appeal to my boss's good sense, "I'm burned out. I need a week on a beach somewhere. I need margaritas and hot muscled pool boys offering to rub lotion on my back. What I do not need," I pause for effect, "is to rush off to some remote middle-of-nowhere small town to investigate some kind of medical scam."

John isn't budging. He's like a dog with a bone. *I'm so tired that even my metaphors don't make any sense.* "Admit it, Lana. This is fascinating stuff. In the last year, dozens of single women have moved to the small town of Goat, Oregon, all because a pair of doctors are running some kind of sex clinic, with promises of 'happy endings.'" He does air quotes when he says 'happy endings' and his eyebrows rise comically high. "Don't tell me you're not interested in figuring out what's going on."

"I'm not interested in figuring out what's going on," I reply flatly. "Insurance scams are a dime a dozen, and they're boring. Come on, John. The Astoria Yacht club is celebrating its hundredth anniversary this weekend. Let me cover that."

John rolls his eyes. "That's a fluff piece," he replies. "It'll be a bunch of rich guys in their boats, sipping martinis and what not. Mindy can handle it."

Lucky Mindy. "You ever stop to think I might want to find myself a rich guy in a boat?"

He snorts. "You'll be bored in ten minutes being some guy's arm candy. Besides, I'm watching out for you. You'll need to infiltrate the community before you can set up a sting at the clinic. That'll probably take a month or two. Think of it," he adds persuasively, "as a vacation."

It's not a vacation, not if I know John. I'm pretty sure he'll be expecting me to write an article a day while I'm hanging out in Goat.

You could always say no.

But then what? Investigative journalists are being laid off by the dozens. I'm lucky to have a job at The Torch. Several of my classmates are flipping burgers and writing freelance click-bait articles for ten bucks a pop.

Of course, click-bait sells, and that's precisely why John's so gung-ho about this story. It involves doctors, sex, and threesomes in a small town. I bet you anything that John's fantasizing about exploding subscriber numbers. "Fine," I sigh. "What's my cover?"

Now that he's ensured my cooperation, John's all smiles. "You have a reservation at the Nanny Goat Bed and Breakfast for the next eight weeks," he says cheerfully. "They're expecting you tomorrow night. Your cover story is that you're a writer working on your next novel."

Goat, Oregon. Nanny Goat Bed and Breakfast. I'm sensing a theme here.

"Tomorrow is Saturday, John. You have *got* to be kidding me."

He spreads his arms wide. "I don't want to get scooped

on this, Lana. This story is going to be big. I can feel it in my bones."

Shaking my head, I get to my feet. If I'm supposed to leave tomorrow, I have laundry to do.

LATER THAT EVENING, I head out to meet my friend Hailey for drinks at a bar in Concordia. We settle down in a booth, and the waiter appears to take our food orders. Once we've been assured of nachos and beer, Hailey looks at me with a raised eyebrow. "What's with the long face, babe?"

"John wants me to check out a couple of love doctors in some crazy-ass small town," I mutter gloomily. "So much for the Astoria yacht club feature I was hoping to do."

She cocks her head to one side, looking remarkably like a parrot in her bright green t-shirt and crimson red pants. Hailey never met a color she didn't love. "Love doctors?" she asks. "Crazy-ass small town. I'm intrigued. Tell me more."

Our beers show up. I drain almost half my glass before answering. "According to John, there's a pair of doctors in the town of Goat, Oregon that specializes in getting women off as part of their treatment. John called it a 'happy ending.'"

She snorts into her beer. "Goat, Oregon?"

"Yup." While my clothes were drying earlier, I had time to do some research on the remote community. "It was founded almost sixty years ago by a reclusive millionaire who wanted a secluded place where he could stash his mistress. His fifteen-year-old mistress."

"That sounds lovely." Unsurprisingly, Hailey's voice is sarcastic. She's the editor of a feminist magazine called Girl Power. Stuff like this outrages her.

"Don't worry; the millionaire is long-dead. The mistress

is still alive though. She's in her early seventies. Her name is Elvira Grantham, and she lives in a mansion on the outskirts of town. I bet you anything that she's a lot more interesting than a pair of doctors with a fondness for pussy."

The waiter shows up at that moment with a platter of nachos, and judging by his scandalized look, he's overheard my last sentence. Poor guy. I make a mental note to tip him well.

Once he sets our food down and makes a break for it, Hailey continues her cross-examination. "So how do the doctors know if a patient wants a little frisky on the side? Is there a form to check off?"

"You're far more fascinated by this than I am." I snag a cheese-coated chip. "According to the anonymous tipster who called The Torch, there's a code phrase. 'Make me feel good, Doctors.'"

Hailey starts to giggle. "This is awesome."

A reluctant smile curls on my lips at my best friend's mirth. "Okay, I guess it *is* kind of interesting, in a strange and demented way. You want to know what the absolute best thing is?"

She nods enthusiastically.

"The clinic is called Clinic of Love."

She bursts out laughing. "Please tell me you're going to become a patient at the Clinic of Love," she begs me. "And you said there are two doctors? Do they both participate in the dirty-dirty? What are their names?"

"Not a clue about the dirty-dirty." I pop a slice of jalapeno in my mouth. "And would you believe the Clinic of Love doesn't have a website? I don't know anything about the doctors."

Hailey leans forward, her eyes shining with glee. "You

should do them," she says. She reaches into her bag and pulls out her ever-present notebook. Flipping to an empty page, she writes a big, bold heading.

Lana's Sex Bucket List.

"What the hell?" I stare at my friend. "You're nuts, you know that?"

"Am I?" she retorts. "When was the last time you had sex?"

The waiter had been approaching us to ask us if we were ready for our next round. As soon as he hears Hailey's loudly-voiced question, his face heats up, and he scampers away. "You scared the kid," I accuse Hailey. "He's going to be scarred for life if you keep this up."

"Please," she scoffs. "I bet he hears a lot worse. You're ducking my question."

How long has it been? I can't even remember. Too long. I'm never home long enough to date someone, and I'm not brave enough for Tindr.

"Exactly," Hailey says smugly.

I roll my eyes. "Hailey, I'm not doing it with the two doctors. Who knows what I could catch?"

"It doesn't have to be dick action," she says encouragingly. "They could pet the kitty, couldn't they?"

"Pet the kitty?" My lips twitch. "Is that what the cool kids call a handjob nowadays?" Before she answers, I cut her off. "Not. Doing. It."

"Spoilsport." She rolls her eyes and writes in her notebook.

1. Say Yes instead of No.

"Really? We're doing this, are we?"

Her lips curl up in a grin. "Of course we are. You're going to Goat. Live it up." She adds a couple of items to her version of my sex bucket list.

2. Have a vacation fling.
    3. And a threesome.

I snort. I'm definitely not brave enough for a threesome. Hailey, on the other hand, seems to act like it's no big deal. "Have you been in one?" I ask her curiously. "A ménage, I mean?"

She's unfazed by my question. "Twice," she replies. "It was five years ago."

Before we knew each other. That explains why I've never heard about her threesome experiences. I rarely talk about my sex life, mostly because I don't have much of one, but Hailey's seldom shy about sharing details.

"I even wrote an article about it in our magazine," she continues. "I got a ton of complaint letters for it."

"Your readers didn't like the raunch?"

"No," she says, with a roll of her eyes. "There was some dick-sucking going on, and readers wrote to me and told me that when I went down on a guy, I was supporting the patriarchy."

It's my turn to laugh. "Some people take the fun out of everything."

"Indeed. But we're not talking about me. We're talking about you and your quest to get laid." Her pen is poised over the list. "What else?"

Flagging down our terrified waiter, I order a pitcher. If we're going to do this, I need beer-induced courage. "Fine. I've never been picked up at a bar."

"Really?" She shakes her head at me disapprovingly. "Lana, you work too hard."

4. Kiss a stranger at a bar.

We drink our pitcher, our voices growing louder as the beer takes effect. I can't stop giggling as we make my sex bucket list. At the end of the night, Hailey tears the sheet of paper and hands it to me. "Cross off every item, kiddo. Make me proud."

I run my eyes down the list we've made.

Lana's Sex Bucket List.

1. Say Yes instead of No.
2. Have a vacation fling.
3. And a threesome.
4. Kiss a stranger at a bar.
5. Get really good oral sex.
6. Have sex outside.
7. Have sex with someone who speaks a different language.
8. Anal.
9. Sex while blindfolded.
10. Threesome!!!!!

Even though I've had a ton to drink, I can see that a threesome appears twice on my list. When I point it out to Hailey, she grins wickedly. "Do it," she says. "When you get back from Goat, I want to hear everything. And Lana? You better not chicken out, okay? You don't know anyone in this town. It's the perfect place to go a little crazy."

Hailey's right. I'll do John's stupid story, but I intend to get something out of the assignment that's been forced on me.

Watch out, Goat. Ready or not, here I come.

∾

Click here to keep reading Her Cocky Doctors!

ABOUT TARA CRESCENT

Get a free story from Tara when you sign up to Tara's mailing list.

Tara Crescent writes steamy contemporary romances for readers who like hot, dominant heroes and strong, sassy heroines.

When she's not writing, she can be found curled up on a couch with a good book, often with a cat on her lap.

She lives in Toronto.

Tara also writes sci-fi romance as Lili Zander. Check her books out at http://www.lilizander.com

Find Tara on:
www.taracrescent.com
taracrescent@gmail.com

ALSO BY TARA CRESCENT

MÉNAGE ROMANCE

Club Ménage

Claiming Fifi

Taming Avery

Keeping Kiera - *coming soon*

Ménage in Manhattan

The Bet

The Heat

The Wager

The Hack

The Dirty Series

Dirty Therapy

Dirty Talk

Dirty Games

Dirty Words

The Cocky Series

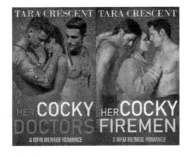

Her Cocky Doctors

Her Cocky Firemen

Standalone Books

Dirty X6

CONTEMPORARY ROMANCE

The Drake Family Series

Temporary Wife (A Billionaire Fake Marriage Romance)

Fake Fiance (A Billionaire Second Chance Romance)

Standalone Books

Hard Wood

MAX: A Friends to Lovers Romance

A Touch of Blackmail

A Very Paisley Christmas

Boyfriend by the Hour

BDSM ROMANCE

Assassin's Revenge

Nights in Venice

Mr. Banks (A British Billionaire Romance)

Teaching Maya

The House of Pain

The Professor's Pet

The Audition

The Watcher

Doctor Dom

Dominant - *A Boxed Set containing The House of Pain, The Professor's Pet, The Audition and The Watcher*

~

You can also keep track of my new releases by signing up for my mailing list!

Printed in Great Britain
by Amazon

64819518R00095